John,

he read. Nobody laughed at the old Dear John joke anymore, but still, Jenny didn't write it.

If I try very hard, I can imagine you here. Long legs sprawled on that lumpy couch in the living room, or sneaking barefoot into the kitchen to eat Oreos and milk in the middle of the night.

This old house seems emptier than ever. The creaks in the floor have forgotten your step. It's too quiet, and you're too far away.

Too far away, a lifetime away. Something tightened in John's chest, something caused by the thought of home and a woman waiting. Fantasy, she had said.

John's life was about black and white, life and death. He didn't know how to deal with fantasy. Her letters had created a past for him and had enticed him toward a future. It might be a fantasy to her, a silly diversion meant to entertain a soldier. To him, a career officer sitting in a tent on the edge of a war, it was a glimpse at a life he had never known. A gamble on a future he had never risked. Not until now, not until Jenny.

A gamble he was determined to try—if he could find this mystery woman.

Lyn Ellis is another wonderful new voice added to Temptation's lineup, and we're very excited to have found her. During Desert Storm, Lyn wrote to an infantry captain whom she'd never met—and thus the seed for *Dear John...* was planted. After the war, she and the captain were still writing, and with his help, Lyn spent four days visiting Fort Riley, Kansas. She had a great time. And while she has no intention in specializing in military romances she does have some other ideas....

Lyn is a professional photographer and has traveled extensively throughout the U.S. and the world. With her camera she learned how to tell a visual story. Now, in her books, she is translating the visual into words, creating memorable characters, vivid settings and compelling romances.

DEAR JOHN...

LYN ELLIS

Harlequin Books

TORONTO • NEW YORK • LONDON
AMSTERDAM • PARIS • SYDNEY • HAMBURG
STOCKHOLM • ATHENS • TOKYO • MILAN
MADRID • WARSAW • BUDAPEST • AUCKLAND

My mom, Emily, who always told me I could do anything.

Manny, who is always willing to help me do anything.

Thanks to all the ladies of GRW for their advice and support, especially: Anne (for loaning me her brother), Donna, Diane, Marcia, Ann and Sandra.

Thanks to the men and women at Fort Riley, Kansas, who were so gracious to me during my time there, especially the Vin-man, Captain Vince Fritton—an officer of the infantry, and a gentleman who sends roses.

Special thanks to the man who started this, then helped it along: Captain John Bushyhead—hero and hellion, and the *real* "Dear John."

Finally, to A. S. Ellis, whose name is on the Wall. The letters are for you.

ISBN 0-373-25588-8

DEAR JOHN...

1

10 September
1615 hours

CAPTAIN JOHN RAYMOND Braithwaite stared at the distinctive pale blue envelope. Real stationery, nonmilitary, standing out like a cool patch of shade in the barren desert he and the men of Delta Company were under orders to defend. He couldn't suppress the tiny wave of pleasure initiated by the graceful handwriting. "P.O. Box 7679, Topeka, KS."

He scanned each sweep of ink, trying to visualize a face and form to fit the sender—to fit Jenny. A series of composite images marched through his mind like a police lineup. A woman with brown hair and dark eyes followed by one with lighter hair and blue eyes. Nothing seemed right.

Too impatient to wait, he flipped the envelope over and carefully pried it open. His hands were dirty from unloading crates of ammunition, and smudges marred the edges of the flap, but he didn't tear it.

"John."

Nobody laughed at the old "Dear John" joke anymore, but still, she didn't write it.

If I try very hard, I can imagine you here. Long legs sprawled on that lumpy couch in the living room, or sneaking barefoot into the kitchen to eat Oreos and milk in the middle of the night.

This old house seems emptier than ever. The creaks in the floor have forgotten your step. It's too quiet, and you're too far away.

Too far away, a lifetime away. Something tightened in John's chest, something caused by the thought of home and a woman waiting. Fantasy, she had said.

John's life was about black-and-white, life and death. He didn't know how to deal with fantasy. Her letters had created a past for him and had enticed him toward a future. It might be a fantasy to her, a silly diversion meant to entertain a soldier. To him, a career officer sitting in a tent on the edge of a war, it was a glimpse at a life he had never known. A gamble on a future he had never risked. Not until now, not until Jenny.

Are you well? Holed up in some dusty corner of a tent on a cot that smells of ancient boots? I've sent a package with batteries and magazines and a few other things you might like. Tell me what else you need, and I'll find it.

What I need is you. Do you remember our trip to Seattle? When you borrowed your friend's motor-cycle to take me for a ride? I was nervous, and you went just fast enough to make me put my arms around you and hold on tight. You were warm and solid, and as long as I could touch you, I wasn't afraid.

The image of her arms around him, her breasts pressed against his back, filled his mind. The desert, the sur-rounding jumble of equipment and men, faded out of existence. He could almost feel the wind on his face, the sense of freedom he always had on a bike. Freedom. Home. It had never seemed so far away, or so enticing. All because of Jenny.

> I'm not afraid now. I know you'll be fine. This whole thing could be called off any day, then you could come home to those who love you. I have a bet with Tina that you'll be home for my birthday. You always manage to surprise me. Your face at my door would be the best ever.
>
> Please take care of your men for their families, and take special care of yourself—for me.
>
> Jenny

John stared at her name for a long time, but couldn't picture her. A tangle of worry and elation knotted his thoughts. He didn't know anything about her except her first name and the images in her letters, yet she seemed to understand him. How did she know all the right things to say? Things he would never admit he needed to hear. Words loaded with wishes and hopes for a future. The kind of words that didn't condemn a professional soldier for being what he was, or for doing what he'd signed up to do.

Take care of your men. How did she know?

"Hey, J.R.!" Captain Wayne Dixon pushed his way into the tent. "I see you got another letter."

"Uh-huh." John's tone was noncommittal as he slid the letter into his shirt pocket. He wasn't about to give Wayne any ammunition to use against him. Wayne might be his best friend, but sometimes he could be a tenacious pain in the butt.

"So, the pen-pal experiment is working out?"

John wanted to curse at Wayne's self-satisfied expression. He got to his feet and moved around the stacked crates that served as a desk. "Yeah. It's just a little weird getting letters from someone you've never met." *And what letters,* he thought to himself. "Are you ever going to tell me who this woman is?"

"Hell, no! Linda would cut me off for good. I promised, and wives tend to keep track of that kind of stuff." Wayne shook his head sorrowfully. "Besides, with your luck it's probably Madonna or Miss Universe—" he smirked "—or General Arlin's daughter. Remember? The blonde who wore that white miniskirt to the parade grounds and sat in the bleachers."

John groaned like a man in pain. "Well, I'll tell you one thing, old buddy," he said, guiding Wayne toward the tent flap. "This female may be coyote ugly and weigh as much as a Bradley—" his serious expression transformed into a wicked smile "—but she gives good letter."

AFTER A DAY CHARACTERIZED by "hurry up and wait," Captain John Braithwaite switched on the light next to his cot. He stretched out, fully dressed, and pulled the blue envelope out of his shirt pocket. He studied the handwriting again before opening it and rereading the lines. The words were disturbingly intimate and yet they were familiar, comforting. Words that hinted at more than friendship—unless his celibate state was beginning to affect his mind. It was the kind of letter a wife wrote to a husband, full of shared history, shared secrets, shared love.

Did she know what she was doing to him? Was she getting some sort of kinky kick out of arousing him? His lips twisted with a smile. Kinky was all right provided both people were having a good time. He could see why she'd demanded anonymity. Who knew what a man might do after reading her word pictures? What a man might want?

At thirty-one he'd lived long enough not to be drawn in by words, or by dreams of a rosy future. But he'd play the game. Words were only ink on paper, and secrets shared with a stranger remained secret.

He sniffed the stationery. No perfume, nothing but the clean smell of home. He folded the letter and slipped it into his private papers, next to two other blue envelopes. Then he pulled out a folder with a pen clipped to one side.

"Dear Jenny," he wrote.

"I PICKED UP SOMETHING for lunch along with your mail." Linda's smile looked a little smug as she stepped through Jenny's front door carrying a grocery bag and two envelopes. "One of the letters is military and it's not Wayne's handwriting."

Jenny glanced at the mail her sister handed her. On top was a plain white envelope with no return address, no stamp, just her name and post office box written in a familiar scrawl. Well, part of her real name. A letter from John.

"I brought you something else, too." Linda waggled a three-by-five photo in Jenny's direction before allowing her to grab it. "Now you can see what he looks like."

Jenny scanned the photograph of two soldiers standing in front of a tank. Wayne, laughing, leaned toward the other soldier as if he was presenting him to the viewer. The name Braithwaite was printed over the soldier's right pocket. Jenny shivered in anticipation.

He was taller than her brother-in-law, his dark hair cut unmercifully short. She brought the picture closer. His eyes were gray or light hazel—hard to tell in the full-length pose. An indulgent smile shaped his lips, and Jenny wondered what Wayne had said to engender that smile. Captain John Braithwaite looked better than she had imagined. Much better. Why didn't a guy like this have someone to write to him? She put the picture aside and opened the envelope.

"Dear Jenny."

She was secretly glad he'd insisted on knowing her real first name. It was the one truth in the fantasy she was weaving for him, with him. The one thing that would always be real between them.

Fantasy. She was getting pretty good at making up new lives, new experiences. After months of lying in a hospital bed her mind thrived on the challenge. Anything to subvert the boredom . . . and the grief.

5 November
2030 hours

All we do here is wait, wait, wait. Compared to anywhere, U.S.A., this place is godforsaken. I received your letter dated the 25th. It reminded me of how much I miss home, how much I miss the things you mentioned. I don't know how to explain it, but I look forward to mail call now. Thank you for taking the time to distract me. I wish I could write letters half as well. I feel like we have an uneven trade deficit.

The military machine here is growing every day. It appears to me that we are committed and we are ready. Everything else is up to Central Command, the UN and the bad guys.

I would like very much to be there for your birthday. You'll have to let me know in plenty of time. You know how I am about dates.

Jenny smiled. He was trying, he really was. Even though he was probably wondering how in the hell he'd gotten mixed up with a crazy woman. A woman who pretended to be his friend and his...lover. Well, John had accepted the rules she'd set. *You know how I am about dates.* Jenny laughed out loud. The sound surprised her. She hadn't laughed in a very long time.

"What's so funny?" Linda asked as she plunked down a plate on the coffee table in front of her sister.

Jenny was still smiling as she looked up. "This letter from John."

"That's odd. The few times I met him, I don't remember him having much of a sense of humor."

"He didn't tell me a joke or anything." Jenny waved the letter toward her sister. "He's trying to humor a crazy woman by going along with the game."

"Well, I don't blame him for thinking you're crazy," Linda teased. "It wouldn't hurt you to have a normal male-female relationship. You're twenty-eight years old and just because you were married to a jerk for four of them doesn't mean you have to keep every other male at arm's length. No. Not even arm's length," she added. "Leave it to you to try half the planet's length. Nobody says you have to marry John, but it wouldn't hurt to at least tell him your real name."

The vision of signing her name—Jennifer Reardon Teale—to divorce papers shimmered in her mind. Jenny's smile faltered. She had barely been able to sit up at the time. A nurse had had to hold her and help her end her marriage. "No, if I do that then I would have to worry about what I said and how I said it. I'd have to dread the day he said, 'Why don't we have lunch or go to a movie?' I'd have to dread the look in his eyes when he finally met *poor* Jenny Teale."

Her sister gazed at her for a long moment, then motioned toward the table. "Eat your sandwich, *poor Jenny,* before you make me mad. You look a damned sight better than poor to me, and I'm grateful you're alive, even if you're not.

"And on top of that, you're going to be rich from the insurance settlement," Linda chided with little sympathy. "One point two million dollars is nothing to sneeze at."

Jenny shrugged. The money just didn't seem real to her. How could she get excited over a settlement when the accident had cost her more than money could ever replace? It had deprived her of the freedom of movement and her job. Someone who couldn't run made a poor regional sales rep for an athletic shoe company. It had cut short any possibility of salvaging her marriage, because her husband, whose life was defined by his athletic ability, didn't want an invalid for a wife.

And it had ended the life of her baby.

Was there enough money in the world to cover that? To make it all better?

"I'm not going to think about the money. I just want to get back to normal." Jenny ran her fingers along her damaged thigh. "Or as close to normal as possible."

Later, after Linda had left, Jenny shrugged out of her robe and sat on the bed, John's open letter in her hand. She always read them several times before she wrote back, before she conjured her next fantasy. Handling the paper he'd handled, studying the way he formed the words allowed her to believe that she knew what he wanted to hear.

He'd been thrust out into the world to fight, while she had been hidden away in a hospital room. They both could use a little cheering up.

Christmas is coming, John, she thought to herself as if he could hear. *What would you like for Christmas? No war? That's what I'd like. I would like you to be home safe and sound. But until you are—* her fingers smoothed the plain white paper *—you're mine.*

2

18 January
2200 hours

Dear Jenny,

I'm sorry for the delay in writing. We've been moving and there just aren't enough hours in the day. You'll also have to excuse my handwriting—I'm holding a flashlight.

I want to thank you for the box of goodies you sent for Christmas. A lot of the men didn't receive anything, so we made use of every item. The only things missing were pictures, but I know how you feel about that.

So far we're still waiting, staring at empty desert (empty except for sheep and soldiers) and wondering how many eyes are staring back. I never thought I would miss the boredom of the support base in the rear, but I confess I miss hot showers and real food.

Your last letter sounded different from the others. Please don't worry. It helps to know you're thinking of me, of all of us. Yet no matter what happens, we are here to do a job.

JOHN REREAD THE LETTER one more time and made a couple of corrections, crossing *t*'s and adding forgotten commas. Then he signed his name. He frowned at his tangled handwriting and realized he'd been spoiled by typewriters and word processors. None of those niceties out here, sitting on a water can somewhere near the border of no-man's-land. It was okay, though. He was sure Jenny wouldn't mind the dirt and the corrections.

He raised his eyes and looked around the makeshift camp. What was going to happen to them when the chest-thumping enemy came out to fight? How many of his men would go home in body bags? Or worse, how many would be wounded or disabled and forced to fight a different kind of war in a hospital?

He knew all about hospitals. He'd learned about suffering long before he ever joined the army. And now, as an officer, he'd been briefed on the bad news. Command was braced for high casualties, for gas attacks and suicide missions—for everything the other side could throw at them. When it started, it was going to be like a tour of hell and these men, *his* men, were going to be among the first to feel the fire.

John carefully folded the letter and stuffed it into an envelope. He needed to get some sleep. If only he had a picture, maybe he could lie down and dream about home, about Jenny.

"ARE YOU WATCHING CNN?" Linda's voice sounded small and strained over the phone.

"Yes, I can't seem to turn it off." Jenny felt as if she should be doing something, but all she could think about was bombs falling and people dying.

"Even though Wayne's not in it yet, he's out there somewhere. I'm not sure I can stand this."

Jenny wanted to say, you can stand it, you're strong and so is your husband. But the words stuck in her throat. How did anyone know how much they could stand until the breaking point came along? She hadn't— until the day she'd taken a tumble with several tons of concrete. She'd survived, but there was much damage. Not just physically, but in other ways that floated to the surface of her thoughts when she least expected it.

The good news, Jenny— her therapist's words after a particularly grueling day of work echoed in her mind —*is that you're alive.* He'd winked at her then and added, *And where there's life, there's hope.*

"Write to him, Linda. Tell him you love him and his sons love him. Tell him you're all right and that you can stand this because he's standing it."

"I know, I know. But I'm so scared—"

"Think of him coming home. Maybe the air strikes will end this thing before it starts."

Before she switched off the bedroom lamp, Jenny reached into the drawer of the night table and pulled out John's letters and the photo. She stared at the picture, trying to reach the mind behind the image, to send him thoughts of hope and safety. On a whim, she pushed the letters and the photo under the cool texture of her pillow.

The dream was like a steamy summer movie shown in the darkness of her mind. Not about war and killing; it was love and pleasure and lust. Jenny turned on her side and pressed her face into the pillow. She could still feel his hands on her, warming her skin, bringing her body to life. By all logic the face and hands should have belonged to Randy, been the memory of how he had touched her when they were newly married—before he succumbed to the lure of being on the road with the team and the charms of the roadettes. *Sorry I didn't call last night. I was beat after the game . . . had a couple of beers with the guys . . . fell asleep. . . .*

Before she wasn't perfect anymore.

It had been so long. So long that she had forgotten the pure animal gratification of two bodies straining in unison toward one inevitable conclusion, for one brilliant lightning strike of pleasure.

She opened her eyes. Her bedroom was as bright with morning light as her body was warm with long-denied urges. She felt alive and vital and wanting. She should have been wanting Randy...but she had dreamed about John.

Her first impulse was to write him and tell him, to share the fantasy. Would it be pleasure or torture for him? Or would he think she'd gone over the edge? *Letter sex.* Jenny sighed. Maybe she *had* gone over the edge. The other fantasies were made up. This one was real. She wouldn't have to invent the words, only write them down.

John,
The sheets were cool around my body, reminding me that I was alone. My mind drifted away, almost too far to turn back. Then strong hands moved upward along my arms to my shoulders, and I realized I was naked. The cool sheets were warming, heated by another body. I wanted to press myself to that heat, to give myself over to the feeling, but I was afraid to disturb the illusion. I didn't want to wake up.

Long fingers traced my neck and pushed into my hair. A face shaded by darkness bent over me. I could feel the stirring of breath against my cheek. Every inch of my skin seemed at once completely awake and yet pleasantly dreaming. I smiled into the darkness.

The hand in my hair started to pull away, intent on other directions, but it became tangled. I heard a soft laugh close to my ear. A laugh of pleasant defeat.

In that moment I knew it was you. I felt that wherever you were, whatever you were doing, part of you was reaching out to me, touching me, warming me.

The tangle of fingers and hair twisted tighter, angling my face to receive. Then your mouth found mine, covering, teasing, drawing forth my need with your tongue. God, you have a great mouth. My lips opened beneath your kiss like a blossom under the persistent probing and tasting of a hummingbird.

I wanted to be kissed for the rest of the night, for the rest of my life, but you wanted more. Although every time you pulled away, you came back to taste and to tease.

My body understood your hands even when my mind was captivated by your mouth. Your fingers smoothed and tickled, finding all of what you used to call your favorite places.

Even caught up in the dream—the ever-growing spiral of feeling—part of me missed your laughter, the look in your eyes when you slip beyond teasing and the playfulness coils into a hunger that has to be satisfied. As long as I breathe, your hunger will find a matching need in me that I cannot and will not deny.

You are so good with your hands. My own fingers seem inept and fumbling as I try to reach beyond my pleasure to touch yours. There is so much I want of you. Time slips by as I answer your tongue with my own. I wish for more than dreams even as this one grows heavier, sweeter. I can feel the muscles of your back as you shift over me. The solid weight of your body seems real, more real than the emptiness I have known without you.

Please, I want . . .

Then I am filled. You are pushing inside me, entering my world, my body, with the gift of your warmth, your strength. Your love. For we are truly making love. No matter how much distance ranges between us, the bodies fit, the pleasure is hot and real, the need urgent.

I feel as if I've never been touched until this moment, yet everything about the shape of you, the smell of you, the sound of your passion echoes through my skin and reaches familiar ground. I have loved you. I have lain beneath you and cried out in ecstasy. I have had you deep inside me.

The feeling is building again, the sweet friction . . . I can't think, can hardly breathe. Don't stop—don't ever leave me again. Please I . . .

I woke up warm and liquid with your passion. I felt beautiful and well loved. Even though I'm alone, you have touched me and pleasured me and given me the strength to face the days ahead without you.

JOHN STARED AT THE PAPER like a blind man, his thoughts a tumbling swirl of confusion. Hot, hand-trembling confusion, nothing calm and cool. His blood pumped faster as his body reacted to the words, yet his mind resisted. He had no idea what to feel or do, and he had stepped a long way past proper. He was tired and dirty and horny and then this letter...this incredible letter. Was this woman crazy, or what?

I almost didn't mail these pages and by now I'm probably wishing I could take them back. If you are offended, or unable to deal with me and my illusions, simply write and tell me to stop.

Jenny

Tell her to stop? That was one thought that had never entered his mind. He wanted her letters, needed them, and he needed to tell her everything, just in case. In the next week, or the one after, they were moving forward. The ground assault was imminent and Delta Company would be in the first wave attacking the enemy's front line, which was carved into the desert between the populated foothills and the cool blue of the sea.

And here was Jenny, weaving pretty civilian dreams for him, *hot* civilian dreams, and it made him want to put his arms around her, to make some of those dreams come true. He was surrounded by over a hundred dirty, grumbling, nervous soldiers, and she was alone.

4 February
0500 hours

Jenny,
Don't stop. I can truthfully say that you have my undivided attention. I can say that I've lost some sleep trying to figure a way to tap into your dreams. I can also say that every time I read your letter I have a hard time concentrating on anything else. Not a difficult time, a hard time and I like it. It reminds me I'm alive, and male, and that there is something be-

yond sand and flies and living in holes. Please don't stop.

The days are ticking off toward a ground assault. As a matter of fact, after this letter you may not hear from me for a while. Some of the guys had the opportunity to call home. Since I can't call you, I'll say that if anything happens to me I want you to know that you made a difference beyond supporting the troops. You made a difference to me.

I've never claimed to be a particularly nice guy. I've done some things and hurt some people, which I regret. But I have achieved a sort of peace with my past and hope that if nothing else, my death will be a final payment to my country for all the opportunities it has given me.

The most difficult part for me in this war is worrying about my men. I don't want to come back whole and alive if half of them are chewed up. They deserve more than a choice between a body bag and a wheelchair.

Some of them are just kids—they still have zits. Over here I'm their mother, their father and their next-door neighbor's pit bull. I feel the gap of age and experience when I talk to them about motivation and commitment. And we are committed. There is no turning back. I have no illusions about what we face. The game of war is insane, and we're now on the playing field.

Take care of yourself, Jenny. You are special and my thoughts are with you. Don't stop.

John

John,

Now I'm afraid. I have tried not to be, but I know

how it is to battle for your life. To fight because everything that used to be so easy is suddenly harder than you ever dreamed. Fight, John. Fight for your country, for your men. Don't spend the precious value of your existence, your future, without exhausting every means you have to protect it. You are part of me now, part of my battle—and I refuse to let you go.

I need to hear your laughter, to scrub your back, to watch you sleep. I need to hear all about your days and share the hours of your nights. I want to watch you grow old and still be your love.

Fight, John, for your life, for our life. Come home to me.

Jenny

3

"IT'S OVER, JENNY! Wayne just called, it's really over!" The tearful joy in Linda's voice was contagious. Jenny swallowed and felt moisture gathering in her own eyes as she listened. "They're coming home."

"John—"

"Is fine," Linda interrupted. "They're waiting for final orders but they've been over there longer than most of the others. Wayne said to keep writing until they have a firm date, though."

Keep writing. Jenny thought of John and what she had to do now. She would keep writing, long enough to get him home, to put some emotional distance between them. It would be like weaning them both from a pleasant drug, the way she'd been slowly taken off painkillers at the hospital. Because it wasn't reality. And after months of sadness and struggle she'd learned more than she ever wanted to know about reality and emotional dependency. One was a rock-hard fact of life, the other was as illusive and addictive as opium smoke. She would never allow herself to be dependent on anyone again.

It hurt too much.

All she had to do was convince John. It would be an accomplishment, like last week when she'd tossed away one of her crutches and now worked, with her therapist's help, toward being free of the other. It was time to get on with her new life and for John to get on with his. At least he was safe and whole.

John,
I'm so glad you and your men are safe. This entire
country breathed a sigh of relief when they tele-
vised the surrender. I know you're glad it's over....

John felt a barely discernible pang of confusion. These
were like the words of a stranger. Where had his Jenny
gone? What was going—?

Suddenly he knew, as surely as if she had broadcast the
meaning directly into his brain. She was backing away.
She had done her duty for the war effort and now she was
quitting. War's over. John was inexplicably furious. He
pushed to his feet and went to find his good buddy, Captain Wayne Dixon.

He cornered him outside the duty office. "Wayne, tell
me who this woman is," he demanded.

"No way, J.R. Besides—" Wayne's snide smile sig-
naled the arrival of his not-so-funny humor "—what if
it's a man?" Wayne guffawed at the possibility. "The
perfect joke on you."

John realized he had one page of blue stationery
clutched in his hand. He shoved it in Wayne's face as his
other hand came up to grab the front of Wayne's shirt.
"I know it's a woman," he said gruffly. "Only a woman
could write what she has. Now, I want to know her *real*
name and her *real* address."

John's urgency wiped the smile from Wayne's face.
"What do you mean?"

"Am I speaking Arabic? I mean she's quitting. She's
going to stop writing, and I'll never know who she is."
John stared at Wayne as serious as death. "You're going
to tell me."

"I can't."

"Why? Because of a stupid promise? For Christ's sake,
Wayne, I'm not some serial killer who's gonna track her

down." He released Wayne's shirt and ran a hand over the stubble of his hair. "I just want to meet her—to thank her." To put a face to the words, he thought to himself. To exorcise the willowy blond vision his lecherous imagination had formed by meeting three hundred pounds of reality.

"I'm sorry, man," Wayne said. "I gave my word. I'll ask Linda, but I don't think she'll agree. You don't understand the situation."

"HE WANTS TO KNOW WHO you are, Jen. He got on the phone and asked me himself. Why can't you—"

"No," Jenny answered with absolute conviction. She could feel heat moving up her neck. "I can't. You don't know what I wrote to him, you don't know how it made me feel." She looked into her sister's worried eyes. "I'm just beginning to feel whole again. I'm not ready—"

"He only wants to thank you."

The heat under Jenny's skin flamed hotter. *Thank me for what?* her mind taunted. *Letter sex?* John wanted to meet the illusion, not *poor* Jenny, not the real woman who held the pen in her hand. "No," she whispered, nearly strangled by the image of how he would react if he saw her struggle with the simple act of walking.

Poor Jenny. Randy had looked at her that way. He'd calmly listened to the doctors when they'd said she would never walk again, never have children, never be normal. Then he'd left. For better or worse, she was not going to volunteer for that kind of pain ever again.

4 April
1530 hours

Dear Jenny,
I know I have no right to ask you for anything.

You've already done more than most. And I don't want to complicate your life or pay back your kindness with aggravation. But I wish you'd be there. You know when we're coming in. Please . . . just be there. I would like to meet you and thank you in person. And most of all complete the cycle of what we began seven months ago.

This will be my last letter before we redeploy. I won't say goodbye, not yet. Please, be there if you can.

                                                            John

23 April
1750 hours

SURROUNDED BY what appeared to be utter chaos, John watched as his men queued up to check in their sensitive equipment. By the looks on most of the faces, army procedure was the last thing on their minds. There was a saying in the infantry about returning from the field. "First you get laid, then you put down your bags."

"Come on, men, you know the drill. The sooner we get this equipment accounted for, the sooner we get next door." Even as he prodded them, John glanced out one of the open hangar doors toward their objective. After flying ten thousand miles, changing planes twice, then riding on buses for another forty-five miles across the flat green plains of Kansas, they were home. Marshall Field, Fort Riley. Only one parking lot separated the two huge metal buildings; only about a hundred yards stood between these men and their families, between himself and Jenny.

Delta Company entered the hangar in single file and stood impatiently beneath a huge American flag suspended from the roof. The speeches were blessedly short, the band a little off-key, but loud. When the formation was dismissed, the babble of joyous greetings and exclamations flowed around John like currents of a rushing river. His shoulders were pelted with confetti and crepe paper streamers. His gaze zigzagged from one hugging couple to another until someone he knew from Headquarters stopped him to shake his hand. Soon he was walking again, moving through the crowd, searching for a woman alone, for Jenny.

John spotted Wayne just as his wife threw her arm around his neck. She hugged Wayne fiercely, nearly squashing the younger boy she was carrying between them. Wayne's other son was plastered to the leg of his father's uniform.

Would Jenny be as happy to see him? he wondered. Happy and warm and willing—

The hand of a stranger pounded John on the back, banishing his feeling of isolation. After shaking another hand, he turned his attention once more to finding Jenny. He moved in Wayne's direction.

When he stopped again, John was close enough to see the tears in Wayne's wife's eyes as she gazed into her husband's face. Why hadn't he ever slowed down long enough to find a woman who would look at him that way? He glanced away, waiting, searching the faces in the crowd. Wishing... Would Jenny be close? Waiting here with Linda?

"Welcome home, Captain." Wayne's wife stepped out of her husband's embrace and claimed John's attention. She transferred her young son to his father's arms and offered her hand.

"John," he corrected as he enveloped her hand with his own.

"Oh, what the heck," she said, pulling him toward her and hugging him.

He hugged her back, feeling a little awkward. He was touched by her welcome, but he wanted to know about Jenny.

"Is she here?" he asked without preamble.

Linda's hand fluttered in the general direction of the crowd surrounding them. "Yes, somewhere. She told me you asked her to come. I saw her earlier talking to one of the wives over near the band." She linked her arm with Wayne's as one of the boys ran off toward a row of mostly empty metal chairs. John's eyes automatically followed. The child loped up to a fragile blond woman sitting alone. He got a glimpse of long legs in faded jeans before the crowd closed in, blocking his view.

Linda pulled Wayne forward. "Come on, I can't wait for you to see how the boys and I have decorated the house." There was a definite twinkle in her eye. "They got to do the living room, but I took care of the bedroom."

"Just tell me what she looks like," John asked, moving along with them for a few steps. He was beginning to feel nervous. Jenny was here—time to face reality.

Linda's expression changed. He could have sworn she felt sorry for him. *Great*, he thought, *it's worse than I imagined.*

"Dark hair, about shoulder length," she answered evasively. She glanced sideways at Wayne.

"How tall? How old?"

She frowned and continued walking. "Older than me, I think. At least, she seems older."

They were almost to the seats now. John's gaze shifted. The blonde was still there. She seemed totally involved in talking to the little towheaded boy. They looked enough alike to be mother and son.

"Would you like to meet my sister?" Linda asked.

John pulled his attention from the blonde. No time for sight-seeing now, no matter how nice the sights. "What?"

"My sister." Linda let go of Wayne as they reached the seats. The blonde looked up and extended a graceful hand to Wayne. He slowly pulled her to her feet and then into his arms.

Blue eyes, John registered as he heard her emotion-filled voice. "Welcome home, Wayne. We were so worried about you."

Uncharacteristically solemn, Wayne pushed her away to arm's length. "And I was worried about you. You look incredible."

"Thanks," she said with a sad smile. "I look a little different from the last time you saw me." Her eyes shifted uneasily toward John.

She looked scared to death. John blinked, startled— Freddy Krueger he wasn't. What in the—

Linda bridged the gap. "John Braithwaite, this is my sister. . . ."

The blonde took a step and suddenly pitched toward him. "J—Janice," she said, stumbling over her own name and her own feet. Out of reflex, John's hand shot out to grip her upper arm and steady her, a courtesy that immediately felt excruciatingly intimate. He watched her face turn an appealing shade of pink before he remembered to release her. She drew a nervous breath and made an effort to smile as she extended her hand. "Mrs. Teale."

Married, that's typical, John thought. *All the quality women are married.* As he accepted her hand, he looked into clear, tear-sparkled blue eyes and experienced an immediate sense of urgency. He needed to find Jenny. He needed to hold a woman in his arms, face-to-face, body to body. His fingers tightened fractionally. Her hand was warm and soft...and trembling. Improper thoughts rampaged behind his polite smile. He hesitated, reluctant to let go.

"Nice to meet you, Mrs. Teale."

She was still staring at him, the faint pink blush fading from her skin. Short blond hair feathering around her face made her look as fragile as a fairy creature, yet there was strength in her hand and in her gaze. The fear had disappeared, replaced by something he couldn't pinpoint.

For one insane moment he wished she'd been waiting for him, that any second now she would pull him into her arms and say "Welcome home." And truly mean it. If this woman were his Jenny, he'd keep her on her back for a week. And she'd be smiling.

John blinked again, surprised by his reaction. *Pull yourself together, John,* he ordered. *Her husband will probably walk up any second and find you gazing into his wife's eyes like some love-struck, hormone-gushing, high school geek.*

"Mommy? Can we go now? I want to show Daddy my new turtle."

"Um, okay," Linda answered. She shuffled the little boy toward the seats. "Pick up your markers and your book."

John withdrew his hand as if he'd been kicked and took a quick glance over his shoulder. "I've got to be going, Wayne." He looked at the blonde, Mrs. Teale, one last time. She was scanning the crowd, a slight frown marring her expression, probably searching for her husband.

"It was nice to meet you," he mumbled before making a hasty exit. He had to get out of there. He couldn't hang around and ogle someone else's wife. He had to find Jenny.

"Welcome home," Jenny said aloud as she watched John disappear into the homecoming crowd. He was taller than she'd expected. And so serious. At least in the photo he'd been smiling: a slow, indulgent smile that had set her heartbeat fluttering each time she'd studied it. Now her heart felt like a sunken stone.

It had been almost a physical pain to be so close and keep up the charade. Now the pain had changed into an ache. She knew it had been an unreasonable hope, but somehow, some way, she had thought he would see through the game. She'd thought if they came face-to-face he would know her, he would see the essence of her letters in her eyes.

Wrong. John had looked right through her, without curiosity, without recognition, without heat. So unlike his letters. The things he had written to her . . .

No. That was fantasy. In person he had been polite but obviously not interested. Untouched by the powerful feeling of connection she had experienced. A connection so strong and immediate she hadn't been able to break the contact. He had pulled away, without even noticing, while she felt burned. Disappointment washed through her, threatening to bring more tears.

Linda appeared beside her with a crutch.

"Amazing," Wayne said as he grasped one of Jenny's arms to steady her. He gestured toward the crutch. "You're down to one now?"

"And counting," Jenny said with a watery smile. *I will not cry,* she swore silently. She had set the rules and John had followed them. He'd walked away from her to go looking for her. The whole thing was ridiculous. So, why did it hurt so much? Why were her rebellious eyes filling with moisture?

"Aunt Jenny, Aunt Jenny." One of the boys tugged at her free hand. "You don't have to cry now, Daddy's home."

Jenny didn't flinch at hearing her real name. John was too far away to hear. "I know, honey." She ruffled the boy's blond hair with her fingers, thinking of John's steady gray eyes. "I'm just happy they're all home."

4

WHY HAD HE THOUGHT she'd be there? Because he'd asked her? What a joke! John stared at the television without seeing the program. All he could see were unknown faces in a crowd. He hadn't found Jenny. He had looked and looked until the crowd thinned out.

The telephone interrupted his angry thoughts. He snatched up the receiver on the second ring.

"Hello." His voice sounded like the one his men heard when they interrupted him for no good reason.

"Hi, John, it's Darla."

John's fingers clenched on the phone. "I recognize the voice," he said, trying to get his anger under control. He hadn't talked to his former lover in over six months, and he hadn't been mad at her then. He didn't want her to think he was mad at her now. He took a deep breath. "So, how are you?"

"I'm fine. I just wanted to call and welcome you home. I read in the paper that your unit was back. Are you okay?"

"Yeah, great," he answered, wincing at the sarcasm under the words. "Fine," he added.

"Was it bad?"

Bad? his mind echoed, stirring up memories. Men slaughtered like animals at the stockyard or herded together to surrender like sheep. Or, waiting for the EVAC, wiping blood and tears off a twenty-two-year-old soldier's face after a land mine had blown his leg to hell. *"What am I gonna tell my wife...."*

John knew nobody wanted to hear about *bad*.

"We didn't lose anyone in our unit, and we did the job," he said, sliding around the question. "It could have been a lot worse." He changed the subject. "How are you and..."

"Steve," she supplied. "We're not dating anymore."

"Oh?"

She laughed. "Listen, I'm having a few people over tonight. Do you remember where I live?"

John hesitated for a moment before answering. He remembered her apartment, her bed. But he didn't feel any enthusiasm for getting reacquainted. He wanted Jenny. He wanted the woman in the letters. A vision from the homecoming celebration, of blue eyes and blond hair—somebody else's wife—haunted his thoughts. He pushed it away. He didn't want to think about another man's wife, he wanted to think about Jenny. "Of course I remember where you live."

"You know you're always welcome." Darla paused. "I'd like to see you again."

The true nature of the invitation balanced in the silence. It sounded like simple, uncomplicated sex, and for a few seconds he let his mind wander toward a long-awaited physical release. The problem, John knew, was that sex was seldom simple and uncomplicated, even with Darla.

"Yeah. Well, maybe I'll stop by later." He had no idea whether he would or not. "Thanks for calling."

John hung up the phone, feeling as if he'd just talked to a stranger. Darla had been what he considered his type: dark hair, dark eyes, divorced. A woman who knew how to take care of herself. Their casual relationship hadn't survived separate agendas, hadn't built a future either of them needed or yearned for. They had been on and off as a couple for nearly eight months before he finally called it quits, yet, right now, he thought he knew Jenny better than Darla, and he had never seen Jenny.

The sudden urge to pick up the phone and heave it across the room taunted him.

His anger mutated into disappointment. He couldn't believe she hadn't come to meet him. What had he expected, fireworks and a happy ending? He should be glad. By not meeting her, he could at least hang on to the fantasy woman he'd created in his mind. A woman of illusion and mystery, beauty without risk and pain, without the realities of life.

For the next few days he would be busy getting his men settled in and refitted. He also intended to find an apartment so he could get his stuff out of storage. He ought to be thinking about what to do with the week of leave he had.

His mind drifted. Maybe he should just go somewhere and lie in the sand and drink margaritas. No, maybe not sand. He'd had enough sand to last a lifetime. Water. Lakes of it, oceans of it.

The specter of unstructured time seemed to stretch out before him like a dark vacuum. He didn't want to spend his leave filling time. He flopped down in a chair and let his head fall back. He thought of the packet of letters he had hauled halfway around the world. If he could spend time doing anything, what would he do? Only one answer came to mind. Find Jenny.

"JENNY, DARLIN', step into my parlor," Drew O'Connell said with an exaggerated leer, his overdone Irish accent contorted into a poor Bela Lugosi imitation. "There are things I want to do to your body."

Jenny made her way through the door toward an elevated table. A fluorescent orange drawstring bag with multicolored patchwork pockets was slung over her arm. "Yeah, and every one of them hurts," she grumbled good-naturedly.

"The price you pay for being a talking, *walking* citizen," he said without the accent. "I see you brought your magic bag—more mutant puppets, I presume." He deftly swept aside her crutch, removed the bag from her shoulder and helped her onto the table.

"I'm currently into giant clams, squid and, of course, dinosaurs."

Drew screwed his face into a patent look of disgust. "Whatever happened to fluffy bunnies and cute chipmunks?"

"Boring, Drew. Borrring. The uglier the better, as far as the kids are concerned."

Drew made a halfhearted sound of revulsion. Jenny smiled. Drew always made her smile. Not that he didn't make her work, but he made it easier to face the pain because he exuded enthusiasm over each increment of her progress. For all his muscles and nonchalant words, he was one of the gentlest people she knew. And one of the most patient. She supposed he had to be; physical therapy defined the phrase *slow process*. But whatever he did worked. She was walking proof of that.

"You got some new sweats," he commented as he began to work the calf of her good leg.

"My sister," Jenny answered. "She's trying to pump up my image along with my muscles."

"Speaking of image," he said, moving up to her thigh. "You promised me a picture for my wall of fame. Where is it?"

"I thought I'd wait until my hair got a little longer, and I gained some weight."

That statement elicited a frown. "This ain't no beauty contest, darlin'." He lapsed back into his imitation of an Irish priest, his voice stern but with a touch of blarney. "This is real life, girl. Besides, you look terrific."

"*Terrific?* The only compliments I get are from a man with a wife and two kids. Why didn't you wait for me, anyway?"

He smiled a crooked, knowing smile. "Don't change the subject. When do I get my picture? Or do I have to bring my Polaroid in here and sneak up on you?"

The last time she'd had a picture taken was with Randy, at a party. The soccer team had won an important home game, and he'd been smiling, full of beer and bravado, his arm hooked around her neck. It had been just before the accident, and he hadn't smiled after that. He hadn't stayed, either.

"Does it have to be full length?"

Drew switched to her bad leg. "Yes," he said without condescension, mercy or any trace of Irish brogue. "Bodies are what this place is all about." His gaze met hers. Jenny dreaded a look of pity. What she saw was something more like quiet anger. "That's what *I'm* about," he continued. "I make them work again, and I want a picture of yours—walking."

Jenny sucked in a breath as he manipulated the damaged muscle and bone of her leg. "Okay, I promise," she panted like a torture victim on the rack.

Drew's smile returned. "I knew you'd see the light."

WAYNE'S HOUSE WAS ten minutes from Post, situated on a street in Junction City lined with other houses just like it—a neighborhood of military families. The kind of neighborhood John didn't visit very frequently. Oh, he was invited often enough, and a home-cooked meal always held a certain allure for a soldier, but discussing kids and mortgages had never been his strong suit.

Most of his peers were married and had children. He admired their courage. John knew from experience how much a family could suffer when fate took over in the place of luck. He knew how much it hurt to watch someone he loved endure pain and accept the fact that there wasn't a damned thing he could do about it.

So, in self-defense, the army had become his family. He had joined for the opportunity to get an education; he'd stayed to serve and defend. Until recently that had been enough. Until Jenny. Until her letters had pried open a battered iron door somewhere inside him and found a tiny vein of hope.

Truthfully, it wasn't only her letters that had started him thinking about the future. Death and war, close up and ugly, had a way of causing one to reevaluate one's life. And John knew the solid plan for his future had shifted under his feet like the sands of the desert he had so recently fought for. Something important was missing.

John pulled his truck in to the driveway next to Wayne's minivan. Kids scrambled from yard to yard, chasing each other or an errant ball. He couldn't remember ever being that young and carefree, even though he'd been the healthy one, the strong one. The "lucky" one. God, what a thought. He shook his head in disbelief as he slammed the truck door. He really was down today.

He should have gone to see Darla last night. He had made it as far as the street in front of her apartment, but he just couldn't get out of the truck and knock on the door. Instead, he'd spent another night alone, another night in a string of nights—in a way of life.

Linda Dixon opened the front door. "Why, hello, Captain." She smiled. "I mean, John. Come in." She moved aside to let him enter. For the first time John found himself really looking at Wayne's wife. She was attractive, smiling and happy now that Wayne was home.

"Is he here?" John asked as she closed the door behind him.

"In the living room. Go on in."

She started to walk past him toward the back of the house but he stopped her. "I'd like to talk to both of you."

Linda suddenly looked wary. "Sure, I'll be there in a second. I have something on the stove." Then her expression changed. "We're going to barbecue. There's plenty if you're hungry."

By the time he and Wayne were seated, Linda reappeared. "We have iced tea, soda or beer," she called from the doorway.

"Beer," Wayne declared, and smirked at John. "Six months in the desert without a beer. I hope I'm not dreaming I'm home."

"Soda is fine for me," John answered. He didn't intend to stay for dinner, so there was no sense getting too comfortable. He already felt like an intruder.

Wayne settled back into his seat like a monarch on his throne. "So what brings you out to our little chunk of suburbia? Did you miss me?"

John felt like squirming but stayed perfectly still. He even managed to smile. "Sure," he countered. "After putting up with you raggin' my butt for months, I just couldn't stay away."

"Uh-huh." Wayne lost his smugness. His expression turned serious. "What's the problem?"

Now that the moment had arrived for John to make a complete and utter fool of himself, the words stuck in his throat. *I want to know about Jenny,* his mind demanded, but his mouth said, "I'm trying to decide what to do with a week of leave."

Linda entered the room carrying a glass and a bottle as Wayne gave a hoot of laughter. "Is that all? You look like you lost your—" The phone rang as he spoke. "Best friend," Wayne finished as he picked up the receiver.

"Hello." After a few seconds all signs of mirth faded from Wayne's features. He sat up straighter in his chair as his gaze found his wife's. "Yes, she's here. Hold on a second." Wayne put the phone against his chest and swallowed before saying, "Drew O'Connell from the hospital . . . It's about Jenny."

Jenny. The sound of her name seemed to slide into John's chest like a blade. Jenny. Hospital. He watched as Linda pulled the receiver to her ear, and realized he was holding his breath.

"When did it happen?" Linda asked. She stared at the wall as if she'd forgotten anyone else was in the room. "I'll be there as soon as I can." After another pause she said, "I know how she is. She doesn't want to be the problem all the time." Linda smiled slightly. "I'll tell her one of the nurses called me. Right, thanks, Drew." She handed the phone back to Wayne. "I have to go to Topeka. Jenny fell. . . ." Her voice drifted off.

"I'll go with you," Wayne said, pushing out of his chair.

"No, hon." She touched Wayne's arm lightly, but her tone was businesslike. "The kids are outside. By the time I round them up and get them changed I could be there."

Wayne frowned. "I don't want you to go alone—"

"I'll drive her over," John interrupted.

Both Linda and Wayne turned to John as if he had materialized from the wallpaper. He watched color warm Linda's features.

"Jenny is my sister," she said, obviously deciding the time for secrecy had passed. "You met her at the welcome-home ceremony."

John remembered feathery blond hair framing a face he'd been unable to put out of his mind. He remembered luminous blue eyes looking at him as if she would fly to pieces if he said, "Boo!" A hollow feeling filled him. Now, after hearing the word *hospital*, he remembered how fragile she'd seemed, and that she'd stumbled against him. He nodded, unable to hide his chagrin. He'd met his Jenny and walked away from her. He should have known, but she was too right, too close to what he'd dreamed she would be.

5

"HI, DREW." Linda's voice was subdued but determined. "I need to know her situation before I go in there."

Drew managed a slight smile. "It's not desperate. The doctor wants her to keep still for a few days, and he's ordered some X rays to see if she shook anything loose." He looked past Linda to John, his gaze stopping on the uniform. "You must be Linda's husband—"

"No," John corrected. "A friend." He glanced at Linda. "A friend of Jenny's."

Drew's smile broadened. "Oh, well. In that case you both should go straight in. She could probably use some cheering up. She brought her magic kit but there's nothing like a friendly face."

A short silence followed. John ended it by saying to Linda, "You go. I'll wait." He saw the relief in her eyes before she strode away.

Drew spoke as he watched her go. "Jenny's been doing remarkably well up until now. I hope this fall doesn't set her back too far." He turned to John, an assessing look on his face. "If you're afraid to see her like this, maybe you should wait until she's back on her feet."

John met Drew's challenging eyes. Friend or foe. "I'm not afraid." It was an automatic reply, an official response to a stranger.

Drew said nothing for a long moment. "Good." His whole demeanor changed, and he awarded John a good-natured grin. "Tell her I'll be expecting her." With a wink he walked away.

HE'D LIED TO DREW. He was afraid.

Was she dying? John paced the waiting room trying to get over his shock. He had stood and listened to a man he had just met talk about a woman he had seen only once. Drew had assumed John knew what was wrong with Jenny, and Linda had hardly said a word during the forty-five-minute ride to the hospital. He was hesitant to push for answers. Was he going to find Jenny only to lose her again? Or to have to watch her suffer?

He stared blindly out the window at the cars in the parking lot below. Not again. He was not going to stand helplessly by a hospital bed, waiting. *Ever* again. The smell of disinfected air seared his lungs as he inhaled. He glanced at his watch. Thirty minutes. It had only been thirty minutes, and he was about to climb the walls.

"There you are."

John turned to face Linda. She wasn't smiling, but she looked relieved. "Is she all right?" he asked. That's as far as he could get.

"She's worried, but as Drew said, it doesn't look desperate. They have one of her legs in traction until they're sure she didn't damage any of the bones. Jenny's hoping to squeak through this with a bad bruise and some pulled muscles." Linda sat on the edge of a couch. She motioned for him to do the same. "We have to talk."

He'd heard that tone of voice before. Here it comes, John thought, something I don't want to hear. He sat down, knowing he was about to face the truth.

"I didn't tell her you were here," she said. "She wouldn't want you to see her like this."

John lost his meager amount of patience. "Like what? What's wrong with her?"

"She was in an accident over a year ago. She was working at one of those high-profile sports-equipment shows at the coliseum in Kansas City. A forklift backed into a wall support, and the wall gave way." Linda looked at her hands. "Jenny was on the second level when the wall came down. She was nearly killed. Her legs, her hip were crushed." She met his eyes once more. "They told her she would never walk again. That she would never—" Her voice caught, but she regained control before continuing. "But she is walking, getting better every week. Until now. . . ."

John sighed and pushed a hand through the clipped ends of his hair. He searched his memory. Jenny had been standing when he met her. She had looked perfectly normal, better than normal, with long legs in soft, faded jeans. The kind of legs a man would ache to touch, to feel wrapped around his own. Then he remembered she'd had said, "Mrs. Teale." Married. That's why she'd insisted on remaining anonymous. A fist of apprehension tightened in John's gut. His Jenny belonged to someone else. Reality stood poised with a sword raised to strike. "What about her husband? Where is he?"

"They were divorced a few months after the accident. He couldn't deal with it." Linda gave John a look that could blister paint from wood. "And if you can't deal with it, I don't want her to know you know."

John simply stared at her, his thoughts fighting each other for attention. Elation . . . then panic. Deal with it? Watching someone else he cared for suffer? One side of his mind balked. *Never again.* He had his personal life in order—no connections, no commitments—and his professional life was committed to the army. And, as far

as the army was concerned, he and his men were certi-
fied heroes. When he completed this command, he himself would be considered hot property, in a position to
write his own ticket—go back to school, choose a new
career track. Did he need to get involved with this woman's problems? He could send her some flowers, thank
her in a letter. He could walk out of this hospital right
now and never look back. She'd never wanted to meet
him, anyway. . . .

The other side of his mind, the one so relieved by the
news of her divorce, wanted to look into those mesmer-
izing blue eyes again. To see if he would find welcome.
To ask if she had everything she needed. To tell her that
her letters had changed him.

Then, unbidden, lines from one of those letters filled
his thoughts. Remembered words of comfort, of hope.
The sound of being alone.

There are only months behind us, and years ahead.
I use the emptiest hours of the night to plan and envision all the things we have to look forward to, then
drift off to sleep with those dreams filling my heart.

She was alone now, lying in a hospital bed. Afraid. He
couldn't let her think no one cared. He cared. Even if he
only saw her once, she needed to know he cared.

"I want to see her," he said.

Linda smiled. "She'll probably throw you out."

An answering smile curved John's lips, although his
chest felt tight. "I just fought a war. How tough can she
be?"

JENNY BALANCED ONE ARM on her forehead and stared at
the ceiling. She had tried to concentrate on the stitches

of her puppets, but she'd simply made a mess. She felt like grinding her teeth, she was so mad. Why had she been so stupid? Drew had warned her about doing too much, about trying to go up those stairs, and now here she was, lying on her back in the hospital. Her nearly healed leg black-and-blue and aching. Guilt washed through her. Someone had called Linda, and now her sister couldn't enjoy her time with Wayne.

She glanced down, over the pieces of felt and the beady eyes belonging to an unfinished puppet, toward her elevated leg. *If I get out of this one, I promise—* The door to her room opened with a swish. Her eyes shifted in that direction as her mind thought of ways to make Linda go home and leave her to her misery. She didn't need a shoulder to cry on. She'd given up on that luxury a long time ago.

Jenny caught sight of the uniform first. Then the face. Her gaze met gray eyes for a millisecond. She couldn't run or even turn and walk away. With a tortured moan of dismay she did the only thing she could think of: she pulled the pillow over her face. Unconnected puppet parts flew in all directions. "Go away, please." Her words were muffled by the pillow, but she couldn't stand to watch him when he looked at her, really looked at her. How could Linda do this?

The pillow didn't block her hearing. She heard as well as felt him move to the side of her bed. If there was a benevolent God anywhere in the universe, he would surely make her invisible. Right now, this instant.

"Jenny."

His voice had a determined note in it. He said her name as if he'd missed the sound of it. Tears stung her eyes; humiliation and a deep regret coursed through her limbs. She threw off the pillow and glared up at him. He wasn't smiling, but he didn't seem shocked, either. Worried? Reluctant? Something was going on behind his level gaze.

Silence stretched the moments into an uncomfortable eternity. Jenny drank in the sight of him, filling in details of the portrait memory had painted in her mind. His face was lean and angular, his nose straight. His mouth, un-smiling now, tightened as if he intended to give her an order. But the intensity in his eyes nearly melted the icy glaze of fear encasing her. She almost forgot where they were, the hospital bed, the fall . . . almost.

One of his hands came to rest on the metal railing surrounding her. "Jenny, I—"

"Not exactly the woman of your dreams, huh, Captain?"

Dreams. Jenny felt herself blush. The content of one of her letters inadvertently flashed in front of her eyes. She saw the memory of it reflected in his.

I have loved you. I have lain beneath you and cried out in ecstasy. I have had you deep inside me.

Why had she brought up dreams? With an oath she put the pillow over her face again. She needed it to hide her embarrassment, to soak up the tears spilling from her eyes. "Damn, damn, damn!"

"Excuse me?" There was amusement in his voice. When she didn't answer he went on. "Actually, I think you might be better looking than I imagined. I can't tell with that pillow over your face, though." One of John's hands tugged at hers. She pulled away but he held on.

"Why are you doing this to me? I'm going to kill Linda!"

He was tugging at the pillow now, and her anger was changing to resignation. If he got a good long dose of *poor Jenny,* he would leave, just like Randy. She let go of the pillow.

"Thank you," John said and tossed the pillow into a chair, out of her reach.

"Why are you here?" she blurted out. John was still holding her hand, and heat seemed to be inching up her arm. She dragged the sheet higher with her other hand.

He leaned an elbow on the railing as if it was a table-top or the roof of a car, not a hospital bed. "I told you I wanted to meet you."

"You did meet me." She tried to keep the disappointment out of her voice, but couldn't. It had been silly to think he would recognize her, but it had still hurt when he'd looked right through her, then walked away.

He frowned as he examined the hand trapped in his. "I know. I should have figured it out. I knew you'd be there somewhere."

Jenny fought her reaction to the warm tingle of his touch. "How could you know? I didn't decide until the last minute."

John looked into her eyes then. She felt the weight of his certainty. "I knew if I wrote and asked you to be there, you'd come." He went on before she could disagree. "As for being here today—" he glanced toward her elevated leg "—I wanted to make sure you were all right."

"I didn't ask you to come." Anger was returning, anger at herself, at her disastrous game. Now she had to hurt both of them, and for what? Some foolish fantasy?

The casual grip he had on her hand tightened defiantly. "Do you want me to leave?"

Tears gathered in her eyes again. Simple human comfort, that's all she wanted. "No," she managed to say before two trails of wetness streaked down her cheeks. "But I don't want you to stay, either."

He stared at her for a long moment, as if he didn't know what to do. The faint humming of the fluorescent light over the bed filled the silence. Finally he propped both elbows on the rail and began to prod each of her fingers with his other hand. A stupid childhood rhyme echoed through her mind. One potato, two potato ... The thought tugged the corners of her mouth into a tentative smile. She brought her free hand up to swipe at the tears on her face.

John seemed to come to a decision, a sparkle of mischief lighting in his eyes. The captain turned delinquent. "Tough, I'm staying." His lips formed the same indulgent smile she had studied in the photograph of two soldiers by a tank. "You want your pillow back?"

Jenny's smile widened reluctantly. "No. I suppose it's too late to hide."

He stretched out the fingers of her hand. "So, is this the famous hand that wrote me all those great letters?"

"Please, let's not talk about the letters." The mere mention had initiated another blush.

"Why not?" He looked puzzled and mischievous at the same time. "It would take your mind off this." He flared the fingers of one hand to indicate the metal, cagelike bed and the sterile emptiness of her room.

"The only reason I could write all those words was because I knew I'd never have to meet you."

"*Have* to meet me?" He feigned an expression of hurt.

"You know what I mean."

"Yeah," he said, growing serious. "I know exactly what you mean. But you did write them, and I certainly read them. More than once," he admitted. "It's what connects us now."

Jenny stared at him, trying to breathe. She could lie and say they weren't connected in any way. Or she could agree and see how long his kindness would last. She didn't want his kindness, or his pity. A rush of fear enveloped her. She flinched and pulled her hand out of his. The movement sent a spasm of pain up her leg. She grimaced. *Relax, relax.* Her mind repeated the familiar chant. She had learned to deal with physical pain; it was emotional pain that still terrified her. Better to face the pain and the future alone.

"You okay?" John was frowning again.

"Uh-huh." She plastered a practiced smile on her face. It didn't seem to fool him; his frown remained. "I'm not supposed to move. This thing—" her hand touched the metal bracing her thigh "—reminds me every once in a while."

"How long do you expect to be in here?" John asked in a tone that demanded the truth.

"The doctors should know something tomorrow. I don't think it will be more than a few days. When I fell..." She hesitated as the memory of the stairs produced another rush of anger. "I mean, I know how it feels when something is very wrong, and it didn't feel that way." She sighed. "I'm hoping my leg's strong enough to take a good thump."

"And keep on ticking," John added.

"Exactly."

"Well, what can I get for you, or do for you while you're here?" His gaze scanned the room as if he was mentally measuring it for a piano. His interest was caught by the bright pieces of material scattered over her bed. His hand moved to pick up an unattached plastic eye resting on the sheet over her stomach.

"Nothing, really," Jenny replied evasively, acutely aware of the two thin layers of fabric that separated his hand from her bare skin. The whisper touch of his fingers skipped across her nerves, setting off alarms. She had definitely been alone too long. She'd never felt so susceptible around a man, not even Randy.

"You must need something, even if it's only someone to play cards with." The offer sounded strained to her.

"Look, Captain...John. I know you're trying to be nice and everything, but you don't have to feel guilty about me. I'm fine. I'm used to hospitals and filling time. I usually—"

"Write letters?" he teased, the delinquent again, although his eyes had lost their amused glitter. He wiggled the beady eye at her. "What is this?"

Jenny swallowed. Why was he making this so difficult? She ignored the first question and answered the second. "It's an eye."

He looked at her, one eyebrow arched.

"For a puppet," she added quickly, and reached for the nearly finished product.

"A pig?" he guessed.

She couldn't stop a grin. "Close." She slipped her hand inside the puppet. "It's a giant clam. I make them for the kids downstairs. It's something they can play with in bed." Jenny suddenly felt trapped by John's meaningful gaze. *Play with in bed.* She clamped her mouth shut. *Will I ever stop saying stupid things?* She'd written him a letter about playing in bed. He had returned the favor.

> There is a game I'd like to show you when I get home. It doesn't necessarily have to take place in a bed. The couch would suffice, or the rug, or the kitchen table, for that matter.

John shifted his relaxed position slightly and smiled a real smile, a charming smile. A smile powerful enough to melt the hinges off any locked door of defense. "So, what do you think?"

Jenny's mind was blank, stuck on the image of her and John on the kitchen table. *Think?* She heard her own voice answer evasively, "About what?"

"I have some leave time, officially starting tomorrow. We could write, but I'd rather talk in person." When she didn't speak, his smile faded slightly. He continued, "Here is as good a place as any."

Jenny's mind was spinning. Was he talking about visiting her? *Think, think! Thinking—good idea.* "Let me think about it?"

He watched her for a moment before his smile disappeared altogether. "All right. Call me." He dropped the errant puppet eye into her hand, then glanced around until he spotted a pad and pen near the phone. "I'll leave you my phone number." He started to write, then stopped and looked back at her. "If you don't call, I'll show up anyway." It was a not-so-subtle threat.

"I'll call." She was already inventing excuses to give him. It wasn't fair. He'd broken the rules. Why did he have to appear and make her want to see him again?

"It was a pleasure to meet you, Jenny Teale." His hand tapped the railing to get her complete attention. "Call me." Then he picked up the pillow and tossed it to her on his way to the door.

IT HAD TAKEN JOHN almost two hours to drop Linda off at home, grab a quick burger in Junction City and get back to his quarters at Fort Riley. There were no messages on his answering machine.

He finally went to bed around midnight. Jenny hadn't called and it irked him a little. Why did she push him away after getting so close in her letters? He punched his pillow a few times before he got comfortable. Was the real man disappointing compared to the one she'd imagined?

Was he disappointed in her? He could see why she'd hidden her identity and her situation. What man in his right mind would get involved with a woman in her condition? He remembered her grimace of pain when she had tried to move. What man would choose a battle he not only couldn't win, but a war he couldn't even fight?

Only a man who didn't know what he was getting into.

John knew exactly what was at risk—the equivalent of emotional Russian roulette—and because of that, he would protect himself by not getting too involved.

His mind drifted back to those ocean blue eyes, eyes a man could stare into for hours, or years. She seemed to have no idea how good-looking she was, even flat on her back in a hospital bed. Angry and sad, all mixed together. She'd said she didn't want him to go, but she didn't want him to stay, either. What was that supposed to mean?

He knew she was used to being alone. Her letters were filled with isolation, with longing. Wanting. Needs that were echoed in his own life. Needs he could understand and finally admit to because of the power of her words. That's why it had been all he could do to leave her.

Hell. He pounded the pillow one last time. He couldn't just say thank you very much and walk out. Especially when he wasn't sure she would ever allow him to get that close again. Well, whether she allowed it or not, he wasn't going to watch another person give up. She needed his help, and he hadn't gotten this far in the military without learning to stay the course.

JENNY LOOKED AT THE PHONE for the thousandth time. Too late to call him now. She didn't know the hour, but the hospital had settled down for the night and the silence loomed louder than the usual bustle of activity. Her room was dim, the curtains outlined by the muted glow of the lights in the parking lot. She felt more alone than ever, tucked away inside the antiseptic walls of her prison.

She looked at the phone once more. She had to be crazy. Why hadn't she called him? It would have been so easy over the phone. She could have simply explained to him that the letters were just a way to pass the time, that she'd never intended to get involved with him, as a friend or otherwise.

He would probably show up tomorrow, just as he'd said, and she'd be forced to say it to his face. To tell him to go away. The thought of seeing him again—if only for a few moments—brought an unexpected rush of confusion and excitement. Why was she prolonging this? It would only hurt more. Her fingers found the switch for the reading light over her head. With unsteady hands she reached for the phone.

John answered on the second ring. "Hello?" His voice was muted, softer, lower than she remembered. He'd obviously been asleep.

Embarrassment prodded Jenny to hang up, but her hand gripped the phone tighter. She could hear him moving, the slither of sheets against skin.

"Hello?" His voice was stronger this time.

All her well-planned words seemed to collide in her throat, derailed by the simple, intimate image of a man in bed. Not any man. John. Her dreams came alive for a flashing second with hot, sweet pleasure. She couldn't have spoken if her life depended on it.

"Jenny?" When she didn't answer, he ordered, "Talk to me, damn it."

"I woke you up." Her voice emerged breathless and small. She heard him sigh. She heard him move again, too. She could envision him looking for a clock.

"What time is it?"

"I don't know. I'm sorry I woke you. I—"

"It's all right," he said. "Why aren't you sleeping?"

"I've been thinking."

"Uh-oh, that sounds dangerous." A huff of laughter turned into a yawn. "Well, I'm awake now, so talk to me."

Jenny gathered her courage in order to say the last thing she wanted to say at that moment. "I didn't really call to talk. I called to tell you not to come here tomorrow."

He didn't say anything for a long time. Jenny could feel her heart pumping against her ribs. Her fingers found the light switch, and she worried it absently.

"It took all night for you to decide that?"

"No," she answered. Her fingers twirled the light switch, and suddenly she was lying in the dark. "It took all night to get up my courage to call."

He sighed again, exasperated this time. "Why are you doing this, Jenny? Your secret's out, and I'm not some slavering animal trying to corner you. Why can't you just let me be a friend?" His voice sent a current of warmth through her. "Don't you need a friend sometimes?"

A friend. She already knew she couldn't be his friend. After the letters, after seeing his face at the homecoming celebration, and after the sense of loss she'd felt while watching him walk away, she knew she was beyond being content with friendship. She had to stop this before her new life was in a shambles around her, the way it had been when Randy left.

"Talk to me. I know you're there. I can hear you breathing." She thought he must be smiling, a teasing smile that shaped the words into an intimate joke between the two of them. She had to cut through the allure before she was sucked in further.

"Listen, I can walk but not without a crutch . . . and after this fall, who knows?" Her voice sounded strident and afraid. She hated that. "Am I the kind of friend you want? A friend who has to be left behind, who can't dance, can't ride a bicycle—" She lashed out at him, at the world in general. All her stupid fantasies seemed even more stupid. "A friend who has never even been on a motorcycle?"

"You're alive, aren't you?" He seemed angry now. "You've got all your parts." He didn't hesitate or give her time to catch her breath. "You know how many blistered bodies I've seen? Men who will never open their eyes again, never see their families. What difference does it make that they spoke Arabic? They were alive one moment and dead the next, and the world went on without them. The world will go on without you, too, Jenny. But can *you* go on? Without the people who care about you?"

Now she could hear him breathing. Hot tears welled up and spilled over her lashes. She wanted to feel his arms around her, to hold on because he was right. She was alive and she did need someone to care about her. And at this moment, she needed him.

It was a scary thought. He'd cared enough about her to answer her letters, to play her games, to find her. And now he was forcing her to choose between her new, hard-hewn rules and her treacherous needs.

"I'm sorry," she whispered.

"Sorry for what, Jenny?" He wasn't going to let her off the hook.

"Sorry for being so stupid, for being so—"

"Hey," he interrupted. "Truce. We're both sorry."

She sniffed to get her tears under control.

John's voice filled the silence. "So what time should I report for duty tomorrow?"

"Duty?" Jenny's concern flickered to life again. "John, I—"

"What time?" When she didn't answer, he continued, "Look, I'm not proposing. No pressure, just friends, okay?"

"Okay," she agreed, feeling overruled yet better than she'd felt all day. "A friend." She could sense a tiny smile rising inside her, angling her lips. Even the mention of duty couldn't spoil it. He wanted to repay her for the letters. Do his duty? Fine. She could accept that much. "How about after lunch, around two?"

"I'll see you then." He shifted between the sheets, preparing to hang up the phone. "Go to sleep Jenny." His whispered words caressed her ear. "Go to sleep . . . and dream."

6

John,
Sometimes it feels as though my life has stopped.
The days pass by without color or joy. The nights
are silent—and long.

I know I'm stronger. I realize I can take care of
myself, as you said I could. But I still believe being
with you is the foundation of my strength. I will
never feel whole without you.

When you come home you can watch all the Sat-
urday-afternoon ball games on TV and spend as
many hours as you like at the lumberyard buying
three boards and a box of nails. I don't even care if
your socks never quite make it all the way into the
hamper.

I just want you here, close enough to touch. I love
the tingling anticipation that any moment of the day
you could walk through the front door. Smiling.

The door is open, and I'm waiting. Missing you.
Jenny

"HOW MANY CARDS are you taking?" John asked, cran-
ing his neck to see her hand. He had shown up in her
room fifteen minutes early, equipped with cards and a
roll of dimes. Now he was seated on the edge of her hospital bed, a suspicious look on his face.

"Three," Jenny announced in self-defense. It wasn't her
fault she'd ended up with four kings in the first hand.
After all, he'd dealt the cards. She gazed at him across

the width of the elevated table between them, feeling elated but nervous. The idea of her and John occupying the same bed, no matter how mundane the reason, made her skin burn. If he only knew—

"That's a relief." John gave her another severe glare that was spoiled by the amused quirk of his lips. "I thought you said you had forgotten how to play."

"I thought you said you were an expert," she replied impertinently. "All that time in the desert with nothing else to do. . . ."

"That's it." He cut through the litany and smiled a humorless smile. "No more mercy."

"Mercy! Are you saying you deliberately dealt me those cards?"

He ignored the question, taking an inordinately long time to adjust the cards in his hand. "Time to put up or shut up. I call." He tossed a dime into the pot and waited.

"Two sevens," she said, slapping down the cards sheepishly.

John's predatory smile made Jenny feel like pulling the sheet up to her chin. "Two jacks," he announced, producing the hand for her inspection before raking the cards together in preparation to deal. Jenny watched his long fingers flip and shuffle the cards. He was wearing civilian clothes, a shirt patterned in blues and yellows and jeans. He'd deliberately rolled up the sleeves of his shirt before they'd begun to play, as if it was a rule for serious poker players.

For Jenny, watching the sure movements of his hands was more entertaining than the game. And of course there was also the fun of scrutinizing his poker face—an expression that hinged on intimidation.

Jenny retrieved her cards when he finished dealing. Three jacks. Unbelievable! He'd won with two jacks in the previous hand. She looked up in surprise, to find John grinning.

"Having a man in your bed seems to bring you good luck," he said, unrepentant.

A man in your bed... The words, in combination with the knowing glimmer in his eyes, produced a head-to-toe shock of awareness. Jenny lost the ability to speak for a moment. She wanted to scold him, to... Before she could get the words out, the door to the room swung inward and Drew entered, pushing a wheelchair.

"Hey, darlin'," Drew called cheerfully. When he saw John perched on her bed, he said, "If I had known you had company, I would have made other plans."

Jenny frowned when she saw the chair.

Drew seemed to read her mind. "Hospital rules, love." He addressed John. "Sorry, guy, she belongs to me for the next hour or so."

John was staring at the wheelchair as if he'd forgotten she was a hospital patient. He seemed distinctly annoyed.

Jenny waved her fingers to get his attention, then handed him her cards. "We'll have to schedule a rematch another time," she said, trying to dismiss him. She had to stall Drew until John was out of the room. She didn't want him to see her struggle to get up. She stared into John's eyes, concentrating on keeping her face free of expression. "Thanks for keeping me company."

"No problem." He glanced from her frozen features to Drew. "I could come back later...."

"No," she said a little too quickly. Jenny thought he looked ready to bolt. So why didn't he go? Drew was snapping the railing down on the side of her bed, as difficult to stall as a speeding locomotive. "Thanks, but I'll probably need to rest after this sadist gets done with me.

I'll call you." She'd promise him anything if he would leave before she was completely humiliated. Drew continued his quest, pulling the sheet down.

John stepped back, rolling the table clear. His gaze followed Drew's hands as they moved over Jenny's nightgown, along Jenny's legs. His jaw was tight.

"Drew—" Jenny pushed his hands away. "If you'll wait a second, I can get up by myself."

The therapist removed his hands and put them on his hips. His eyes fastened on Jenny, warning of a pending lecture, but he remained blessedly mute.

Jenny swallowed to counteract the sudden dryness in her throat. Drew seemed intent on stripping her naked emotionally—and to some degree, physically—in front of John. The very idea of exposing the true extent of her injuries made Jenny's head swim with embarrassment and fear. After a silent, pleading look in Drew's direction, Jenny faced John again. "What time should I call you?"

"Anytime this evening," he answered and finally moved. But rather than heading for the door, he made his way around the bed until he was standing next to Drew.

John extended his hand to her. "Come on."

Great! Instead of leaving, he was intent on helping her. It made Jenny want to scream. She'd been freed from traction earlier that morning, but she had to move slowly and carefully. And there were scars from the surgery she'd had after the accident. At least she was wearing her own gown instead of hospital issue. She tugged the gown lower, over her knees. The longer length and the delicate edging of lace made her feel somewhat more human. Her hand slid into John's but her heart dipped like the downside of a roller-coaster ride. Now he would know everything. With a sigh of resignation she inched her legs toward the edge of the bed. Drew stepped back as John eased her forward.

Don't volunteer, The old military creed came to John's mind as he watched her slow progress. He was suddenly unsure about forcing her to accept his help instead of her therapist's. *What the hell am I doing?* She'd obviously wanted him to go and he'd intended to. Right up until he'd seen another man's hands on her. When she had pushed Drew's hands away, a crazy, primitive urge had plowed through John. He didn't want anyone else touching her, helping her, taking care of her. He wanted her to depend on him. When she reached the edge of the bed, John heard Drew's voice behind him.

"Brace her on the left side."

John stepped to that side and slid his arm around her waist. *Have you completely lost it?* his brain screamed. *Don't start something you can't stick around to finish.* His fingers tightened against the thin cloth of her night-gown and the warmth of her skin sent a surge of response up his arm. The forwardness of what he was doing surprised him. They had never been together in a normal getting-to-know-you situation, yet here she was, dressed in her nightgown, with him touching her as if she belonged to him. As if he'd held her like this a hundred or maybe a thousand times before. He only knew that he had to make sure she wasn't hurt, that she wasn't afraid.

Her eyes were nearly level with his and for a moment he couldn't focus on anything but her surprised blue gaze. Then her face. Her pale skin, tinted with pink, was so close, close enough to touch, to kiss. Her hair smelled sweet, like apples or apple blossoms, not like hospital disinfectant. He wanted to push his face into her hair and breathe.

Then a melancholy expression crossed her features and she turned away. She'd been smiling earlier, smiling and beautiful. Now . . .

John felt like swearing.

"Hang on to me," he said, returning to the task at hand. She placed her arm across his shoulder and her fingers gripped the thick cloth of his shirt. A vivid image invaded his mind—of another time, of other hands gripping his strong arms, of helping someone into a hospital bed rather than out. Sorrow surged past logic. Damn! He was determined not to think about the past anymore. He cleared his throat. "Ready?"

"Ready." Her voice sounded lost and sad. He wanted to pick up her slight frame and hold her against his chest. He wanted to kiss her until the sadness inside both of them went away. Instead, he braced her as she slowly slid her feet to the floor.

Drew shifted the wheelchair into the proper position and John settled Jenny into it. She wouldn't look at him, and it made him angry. He planted a hand on each armrest, then lowered his face until she was forced to meet his gaze.

There were tears in her eyes, and a knife of pain slowly twisted in John's stomach. Did it hurt so much to simply get out of bed? He couldn't take it. He had to get out of there. He couldn't bear the suffering, not anymore. He forced a smile of goodbye to his lips. "Call me later?"

She nodded without enthusiasm. John studied her. He couldn't walk away when she looked so distraught, so beaten. Not his Jenny. Without thinking he leaned forward and kissed her lightly on the cheek. The kiss was meant to be brotherly, but it left him breathless. He seemed to be falling forward into this woman's life. And he was unable to stop the momentum. Her blue eyes had darkened with questions. "Talk to you later," he whispered before forcing himself to straighten and exit the room.

"ARE YOU IN BED?"

"Not yet. I was waiting for you to call." John sat on the side of his bed. With the phone propped against his shoulder, he untied the laces of his athletic shoes. He felt good. He'd run until all thoughts of past and future had burned out of his brain. And he had come to a decision. The least he could do was hang around and help Jenny until she could go home from the hospital. He was not going to let ancient history ruin his life. "How are you feeling?"

"Fine. Better," Jenny answered. "Drew talked to the doctor and he says I can probably go home day after tomorrow."

John tossed one of his shoes aside and held the phone steady. His decision faltered. He'd thought she would be in the hospital longer than two days. "That's great," he said, then paused. "Where's home?"

"You don't know, do you?"

John could almost hear her smile, and his lips curved in answer. "Hey, I'm a Ranger. I can find you. We learn all sorts of tracking techniques in the army. If all else fails, I'll follow you when you leave the hospital."

"That's cheating." She laughed.

"Whatever works."

"Speaking of cheating, let's talk about how you play cards."

"Let's not." John kicked his other shoe aside and stretched out on the bed.

"You were letting me win."

"I was merely giving you a head start, ma'am. I'm told I'm one lucky SOB. If you like, the next time I'll simply beat the socks off you."

"I wasn't wearing any socks."

A slight pause followed as John envisioned what she *had* been wearing. A white nightgown with some lace on it. He remembered feeling the warmth of her skin through the thin material. "Well." He drew the word out. "I suppose we could bet on your gown."

The banter seemed to be careening out of bounds, yet Jenny didn't want to stop. He'd kissed her, and the memory had buoyed her through a day of pain and uncertainty. Now she wanted to play, to enjoy the news that she could go home.

"Strip poker with a cheater? Not likely. Do I look like a fool to you?"

"Actually, I think you look beautiful."

Jenny's smile and her urge to banter came to a skidding halt. *Don't,* she wanted to say. *Don't be nice to me, don't make me want to believe in you, or in us.*

"Are you still there?" he asked.

"I'm not beautiful."

"I may cheat at cards, but as an officer and a gentleman, I wouldn't lie." The sensual, teasing note in his voice sent a tangible flutter leaping over all the fences she had so carefully placed between them.

"Yes, you would," she answered, clinging to her sense of humor. "But thanks, anyway." Her mind scrambled for a new topic.

"So, Linda tells me that you'll be giving up this command in a few months. Where are you moving?"

"I'm not sure yet. I'm checking around. What's your address?"

Diverting him was about as easy as ordering a river to change its course. "John, you've already made my stay in the hospital bearable. I think we can call it even."

"What is it with you? Is everything something for something? Don't you get it? I want to see you, to know you. Is there anything wrong with that?"

"No, there's nothing wrong with it," Jenny answered, thinking exactly the opposite. Everything was *too* right—that was the problem. She didn't want to start taking this whole thing too seriously. Maybe she should end it now. "It's just that we're going in different directions." His future was wide open, hers had been redefined forever. "You'll be changing commands and I plan to move away."

"*What?*" The one-word reply vibrated with shock.

"I'm moving, probably by the end of the year," she continued, adding to the logical speech she'd composed in her mind. Better to have everything out in the open. Well, she vacillated, almost everything.

"Where?"

"Oh, I don't know. I, uh, I'm getting some money from the insurance settlement. I just want to get away from here . . . start over somewhere else. Maybe Oregon or Washington State."

He took a moment to digest her answer. "Are you sure it's enough money to reestablish yourself? I know how it is to move every few years. On a budget—"

"It's enough," she said, cutting off his advice. Why had she brought up money? she wondered, although deep inside she knew. Because the money was her escape from a lifetime of dependency, and she wanted him to know she wasn't helpless.

He seemed to take the hint, but didn't drop the subject completely. "You'd really move halfway across the country? Away from your sister and her family?" His tone was censorious.

Jenny felt her anger stir. She could look after herself. "Linda needs to take care of her own. She shouldn't spend her life worrying about me."

"Who *is* going to worry about you, then?"

"Nobody, and that's the way I want it. I'm tired of being the problem, the disappointment, the one who always needs help." She didn't want anyone to sacrifice their happiness in order to take care of her.

"Is that how you think Linda sees you?" Now he sounded angry.

"Well, no, not exactly, but I'm sure she would be relieved if she didn't have to run back and forth from Junction City to Topeka to check on me all the time."

"Maybe she wants to do it—because she loves you."

Jenny sighed. He would never understand. It had nothing to do with love. Love was ethereal and illusive. Dependency and not being normal were reality. Jenny knew that, and she could deal with it. "I know she worries about me. I'm family. But even sisterly love can wear thin."

John abruptly changed the subject. "So, you live in Topeka? What's your address?"

"I just explained why we shouldn't—"

"I know, we only have a short time before both of us move on. We should make the most of it, right?" The words were clipped and to the point, like a challenge.

Jenny had to fight her rising anger. The urge to let go and yell, "Leave me alone. I have this all figured out!" crowded her throat. Instead she tried to explain once more. "That's not what I meant—"

"What's your address?"

"It's 288 Sycamore!" she shouted before she realized she'd given him exactly what he wanted.

7

JOHN UNLOADED THE LAST three boxes of his belongings, which had been in storage since before the war, then surveyed the disarray.

In deference to his unsettled life-style he didn't collect a lot of extraneous possessions. What he owned was utilitarian and basic, with the exception of a state-of-the-art music system and a few mementos of his military travels—a beer mug from Germany and an elaborately decorated knife from Korea. Even so, the empty apartment seemed to shrink with every box. What the heck, he was only one person.

A cold, wet nose pushed against his hand. He chuckled and shook his head, amending the statement. He was one person—with a Labrador retriever for two weeks.

John ruffled the short fur on the dog's head and led him into the kitchen to the amenities. Food and water. He watched as Deeno rooted around noisily in the dry dog food, as if he was checking its authenticity, and wondered how he'd gotten talked into Deeno-sitting. If this dog wasn't housebroken—as his buddy Nick had promised—then Nick had better stay on temporary duty. Otherwise, he'd have to face an extremely pissed-off captain.

John looked at his watch. A quarter after three. He was bored with unpacking, he'd already taken Deeno for a walk and it was too early for his own run. He leaned against the kitchen cabinet as he thought of the subject he'd been trying to avoid.

What was Jenny doing? Maybe he should call her, check on her. No. He crossed his arms in defiance. He had plenty of other things to do. The last thing he wanted to do on a perfectly fine Sunday afternoon was hang around a hospital. He'd go later this evening, leave at six-thirty just as he'd planned. It would take him exactly forty-five minutes to get from his front door to the hospital in Topeka. Then he could look into those sky blue eyes and—

His feet were already moving. He snatched up his truck keys even as the logical side of his mind reminded him he had only unpacked one box and that several other boxes needed his attention. He was backing out of the parking lot into the street when he realized he'd locked his front-door key inside the apartment, along with Deeno and the duplicate key he'd picked up from the hardware store. He never slowed down. Hell, the manager could let him in.

JOHN WAS SURPRISED to find Jenny's bed empty, the sheets pulled to one side and the railing down. Her colorful bag of puppets had been tossed into the chair near the bed. Worry stifled his annoyance. He wanted to see her. Where was she?

"I think you'll find her down on the second floor," the nurse at the station informed him. "Pediatrics."

Pediatrics? "Thanks," John replied and headed for the elevator. What was she doing in pediatrics?

The brightly colored walls of the hallway told him he'd found the right place. His feeling of dread increased with every step as he followed a painted procession of bal-

loons and bears, rainbows, kittens and ducks to the pe-
diatric-floor nurses' station.

"Excuse me."

The young nurse on duty looked up. John watched her
attention shift from neutral to interested. Her gaze went
from his face to his ringless left hand, then back. She
smiled. "May I help you?"

John stared into the nurse's warm brown eyes, unable
to appreciate the view. At that moment he only wanted
to find a pair of clear blue eyes. "I'm looking for a
woman, uh, Jenny Teale. Short blond hair—"

The interest faded from her eyes. "There's a woman in
205. Um . . ." She glanced down at a chart. "Mark Jami-
son. He's our only patient at the moment. Down the hall
on your right."

"Thanks," John said, moving away.

As he passed room 204 he heard a high-pitched voice
emanating from room 205. "May I stay with you? Huh?
Please, please, puhleeze? I promise I'll be good. I won't
jump on the bed like this, or tickle your toes like this."
John couldn't hear any answer but he thought he de-
tected a giggle. It eased some of the tension building in
his muscles. He could do this.

He stepped through the open door as the voice continued. "And when your sister comes to visit I can bite
her on the ear like this."

Mark's squeal of laughter lifted Jenny's spirits. Ini-
tially it had taken some effort to get him to smile. Now,
however, they were buddies. As she let go of his ear she
saw Mark's eyes shift in the direction of the door. Then
she felt a hand lightly touch her shoulder.

"Hi," John said, and smiled at Mark before looking
down at her. A breathless rush of awareness enveloped
Jenny. John's mere presence in the room set her heart

beating faster. "I wondered if you'd checked out of this pop stand."

His teasing tone didn't match the solemn look in his gray eyes. But Jenny smiled anyway. She'd thought about him all morning, and now she felt as though he'd appeared in answer to a wish.

"John? This is Mark."

"Nice to meet you, Mark." Jenny watched John extend his hand for a handshake. Mark looked very young and very proper as he placed his small hand in John's larger one. John barely closed his fingers because of the IV needle inserted in the back of the boy's hand.

"Hi," Mark said shyly.

John pulled his hand away and rested it on the handle of Jenny's wheelchair. He cleared his throat as if he had something important to say. "So, Mark, are you trying to steal my girlfriend? Or what?"

Mark looked at Jenny with bright eyes and shook his head.

"I'm not your girlfriend." Jenny laughed as she swatted John with the puppet fitted over her hand.

"She is," John gravely assured Mark and grabbed Jenny's arm so she couldn't hit him again. "What is this thing?" he asked, indicating the green-and-pink dinosaur puppet.

"This *thing* is a stegosaurus, and it's a friend of Mark's."

John spent a long moment inspecting the puppet, manipulating Jenny's hand through the fuzzy felt material. "A stego-what?" A crooked smile settled on his lips. "Does it talk?"

Jenny swallowed, captivated by the smile but unwilling to cooperate. No way was she doing her puppet shtick for a grown-up audience. "Yes, he does talk," she replied, pulling her hand away. "He bites, too." Jenny moved her fingers to open and close the puppet's mouth in a threatening manner.

"Well, in that case—"

"Excuse me, folks." A nurse entered the room. "Sorry for interrupting, but I have to take Mr. Mark's vital signs."

Jenny smoothed Mark's hair back from his forehead. "I guess I better get back upstairs." She extracted the puppet from her own hand and placed it on his. The nurse fiddled with the IV, then pulled a blood pressure cuff from a hook behind the bed. "I'll come see you in the morning before I leave. Okay?"

Mark nodded before adding quietly, "Okay."

Jenny rolled her chair backward, out of the way, and glanced toward John. For once he wasn't paying any attention to her. He was watching the nurse put the cuff around Mark's thin arm. The expression on his face was oddly grim.

"You all right, bud?" John sounded as if he was half ready to pick a fight with the nurse.

Mark looked up at him, his face a mirror of male bravado. "Yeah," he answered. "It only hurts when she sticks my finger."

John moved over behind Jenny's chair. "Well, you hang in there. If they give you any trouble, call room 408. We'll send in the Rangers."

Jenny waved goodbye as John rolled her from the room. She was surprised by the easy camaraderie between the soldier and the little boy. John seemed to like kids. When they reached the elevator doors in the hallway, John pushed the Up button but remained behind her, out of sight. She was about to take him to task for calling her his girlfriend when she heard a harsh exhalation of breath. She let her head fall back in order to see him.

John was leaning on the grips of her chair, his head dropped forward, his eyes shut. He looked as if he'd just taken a punch in the stomach.

Slowly his eyes opened and met hers, but he didn't seem to see her.

"Man, it kills me to see a kid sick like that."

Thoughts and words collided in Jenny's mind. Before she could untangle the jumble, the elevator door opened and John rolled her wheelchair forward, causing the two people in the elevator to step back. They rode up in silence. Jenny glanced at John once, but he was staring at the blinking floor indicator, his thoughts obviously a million miles away.

"He's not dying, you know," Jenny said when they were alone in her room. John had pushed her wheelchair to the foot of the bed, then walked past her to gaze out the window.

He ran a hand over the taut muscles of his jaw. "I'm glad." He relaxed slightly. "It just gets to me—a kid with needles feeding him and nurses poking him."

"Some of us need that kind of care to live."

John turned toward her. "Some get that care and die anyway." His eyes were full of anger . . . and pain. He seemed even more uncomfortable. "I'm sorry," he said. "I know you've been through a lot, too. It's just that I—"

He frowned and faced the window once more. "I've always been the lucky one. The kid who never fell out of a tree, the teenager who got knocked off his bicycle by a car and only got a skinned knee. . . ." Jenny saw he was clenching his fists. "The soldier who went to war and never caught so much as a cold."

"You sound disappointed."

He brought one large hand up to rub the back of his neck, then swiveled to meet her eyes. "My younger brother wasn't so lucky."

Jenny found herself holding her breath. He sighed and settled into the chair across from her. "When I see a sick kid, I feel like getting down on my knees and thanking someone—or, at the very least, requesting a transfer of a little of my own good fortune."

"What happened to your brother?" She had to know.

"He died when I was seventeen. He was only thirteen. He had leukemia." John's eyes were glazed, as if he'd gone back in time. "Despite the doctors, the hospital, *everything*...he suffered. And then he died." He looked down at his hands. "It broke my mother's heart."

And yours, Jenny wanted to say. She could feel the sting of tears behind her own eyelids as she watched him wrestle with his emotions. She knew what it was like to lose a child. But she'd never known hers, never had the chance to love it, or been forced to stand by and watch it suffer.

John shrugged stiffly. "Anyway, after my brother, it looked like my luck had finally run out."

"It must have been terrible," Jenny said. "I don't know what I'd do if something happened to Linda. She's all the family I have left."

"You'd do what I did. You'd get up out of bed every day and go on. I had one more year of high school to finish, and because of the medical bills we had no money for college." His pain seemed to retreat, and he met her eyes again. With a twist of his lips that resembled a smile, he continued. "But I managed to get through it with some help from friends and later from the army. I even started to believe in luck again.

"And then the war..." He shifted position, a slight movement of his shoulders. "I saw a lot of people get hurt..." He paused, as if to gauge how much to say. "I saw a lot of people get killed," he amended.

"And you came back, safe and sound."

"Yeah. My men came back. That meant a lot to me. We had a few injuries but no casualties. You know, when we were waiting for final orders before the sweep, I figured my whole life had led me to that place and moment. That all my luck was about to be cashed in. And I was ready. Except for one important bit of unfinished business...."

Jenny fought to control the topsy-turvy sensation inside her. "The letters," she whispered hesitantly.

"Not just the letters. You." He leaned forward, balancing elbows on knees and clasping his hands together. "The woman who wrote the letters."

"And now that you've met me you're feeling guilty because I'm sitting in this chair and you're walking around." It was a statement, not a question. Jenny struggled to brace herself for the truth. Any second he would wish her good luck and tell her he had to get on with his life.

John frowned and trapped her gaze, his eyes betraying blatant interest and a little exasperation. "Believe me, guilt has nothing to do with what I feel when I'm around you."

Jenny was stunned. And suddenly more afraid than she'd been in a long, long time. "But you were just talking about guilt..."

"No. I was talking about the letters, and about luck—" The rattle of a cart sounded in the hallway outside the door, then the door swung open. John's gaze shifted past Jenny toward the woman entering the room.

"Here's your dinner tray," the food service attendant announced. She slid the tray onto the elevated table and asked Jenny, "Do you need a nurse to help you back into bed?"

The emotional tension in the room was so thick that neither Jenny nor John responded. Finally John got to his feet. "I'll help her."

"Okay," the woman said, briskly accepting his answer, oblivious to everything except her meal schedule. "If you have any problems, buzz the nurses' station."

The door slid closed and John stood facing Jenny. After a long moment he stepped behind her and pushed the wheelchair close to the bed. "Better eat it while it's lukewarm," he said in halfhearted humor. Then he offered his hand.

Jenny looked from his long, blunt fingers to his steady gray eyes. She didn't want to touch him. Every time she touched him her attraction to him escalated. And now she knew why he was being so nice to her. Because of his brother. Because someone he'd cared about had died in a hospital. The silence in the room deepened as seconds passed.

"I'm sorry," she said, "about your brother." All the other words she wanted . . . no, needed to say remained jammed in her throat.

"Jenny. . ." John's voice was low, almost a caress.

She watched her right hand rise without any conscious decision on her part. His warm fingers closed around it in a gesture of finality.

Once she accepted his help, he turned brotherly. With a level of efficiency reminiscent of Drew, he helped her back into bed. In a few moments she was facing her evening meal: some unspecified kind of ground meat with mashed potatoes and green beans.

Her appetite had fled. The appeal of hospital food hadn't improved with familiarity, and Jenny's enthusiasm failed entirely when she was required to eat with an audience. John leaned against the window with his arms crossed over his chest. He'd shrugged off the heaviness of their conversation and seemed to enjoy watching her squirm. "Want some?" she asked hopefully.

He made a great show of studying the contents of the tray before shaking his head. "Looks too much like an MRE to me. I ate enough of those in the desert." He smiled. "I'm sticking to real food like pizza and cheeseburgers."

Jenny gave him a pained glare before she hesitantly sampled a piece of the meat. It didn't taste quite as bad as it looked. "This is great," she said with a sweet smile.

John laughed. "Yeah, right." With a grin that made Jenny's stomach do somersaults, he placed a slightly callused palm on her forehead. "You must be sicker than they thought."

She couldn't help but smile back, even though he was touching her again, even though she felt as if a trapdoor had sprung open beneath her and she was falling through space.

Even though she knew, sooner or later, she'd strike solid ground.

"It's a conspiracy to keep us weak and compliant," Jenny managed to quip as John's hand slid away. His hand had felt cool against her skin, and she knew her cheeks must be blazing red.

"I'll have to remember that. I'm not interested in weak, but compliant . . . Now there's a concept."

8

"I COMMAND YOU to take it easy for a week or so," Drew ordered as he pushed her down the corridor in a wheelchair the next afternoon.

Linda kept pace on Jenny's other side carrying her crutches and her bag. As they reached the elevators, Linda pressed the call button and said, "I want her to come home with me, but she insists on staying in her own house."

Drew studied Jenny's face. "She'll be fine at home." Then he spoke sternly to his patient. "No stairs, no acrobatics. Use *both* crutches. Another fall could mean more surgery."

"I know." Jenny sighed. "Believe me, I've learned my lesson. I promise to go slow until I feel stronger."

The elevator door opened, and he pushed her forward. "You'll go slow until *I* tell you you're stronger."

"Yes, Mother O'Connell," she singsonged merrily.

Going home. She was going home and nothing could spoil the day. Not even the fact that she hadn't heard from John. She'd thought he would at least call.

As they left the elevator on the first floor Jenny glanced down the hall and saw two soldiers in uniform. One of the soldiers—Wayne—was holding a young boy in his arms and another by the hand; the other was John.

As Drew pushed Jenny closer, she heard Wayne say, "Now, men." In unison the two tall captains and the two little boys saluted her. She smiled, despite having to blink back the sudden haze of moisture in her eyes.

The older boy rushed to meet her, holding a bunch of daisies. He'd apparently been coached. He shoved them into her hands. "Welcome home, Aunt Jenny."

"Thanks, Tommy." She touched the flowers. "They're beautiful."

"Captain John got them," Tommy said, then glanced back forlornly at his father as if he'd been told not to tell.

Jenny looked at John but couldn't speak. The letters. She'd told him she loved daisies. He had remembered.

"Your honor guard is ready to escort you," Wayne said, putting his younger son down. "By the way, do you have any idea how much pull it takes to get a soldier into a uniform on his day off?"

"Wayne." Linda's voice held friendly warning.

He grinned and shrugged. "I'll get the van."

Wayne went through the front doors while the rest of the group followed at a slower pace. With a smile, John fell into step next to Jenny's wheelchair.

"Pretty sneaky," Jenny said, trying to hang on to her composure. "Infiltrating the family."

John's smile widened. "Yeah, I know. In the army we learn how to get the job done. Failure is not an option."

"Thanks for the flowers . . . for remembering," she stammered, wondering what other sections of her letters he had committed to memory.

Judging by the way his friendly smile turned into a wicked grin, he remembered every word. "You're welcome."

When they approached the van, Wayne opened the door. Instead of offering to help Jenny, Drew stepped back and looked at John. Jenny thought she witnessed a flash of unspoken understanding pass between the two, but it was so quick and subtle she wasn't sure if she'd imagined it.

John helped her out of the chair and into the back seat of the van. Events seemed to be sweeping her along on a relentless current. She was too overcome at the moment to fight. She wanted to relax, to be surrounded by the people she loved. *Loved?* That brought her up short. She stared at John's profile as he took his place in the passenger side of the front seat. She barely knew him.

As if he perceived her gaze, he turned to meet her eyes. He looked surprised at whatever he saw—and interested.

JOHN COULDN'T BELIEVE he was doing this, including himself in Jenny's life as if he belonged there. It seemed as if every time he found the perfect point to stand back and let her go, his feet stepped forward, regardless.

It wasn't altogether fair. She couldn't very well run. Did she want to? He hadn't spent a lot of time seriously pursuing women, so his single-minded pursuit of Jenny amazed him. He felt as if someone had taken over his life and aimed it in a diametrically opposite direction. Why couldn't he walk away from her? Why did even the thought of never seeing her again make him furious and desolate at the same time?

He'd decided to stick around until she was out of the hospital. Now here he was, in the middle of her family and her life, and he couldn't think of anywhere else he would rather be.

"We're going to stop at Tony's for ribs," Wayne said. "I hope you're hungry."

John looked at Jenny. She didn't smile. "I'm hungry," she said, then hesitated. She nervously ran one hand through her feathery hair. "I'm not sure I'm ready for public exposure yet, though." She tugged at the loose top of her pink sweats. "These are not exactly formal."

"You look fine," Wayne said. "We've got a blanket in the back we can throw over your head, if you like."

Linda reached across from the back seat and punched her husband in the shoulder. "Very funny, Captain," she said, putting great emphasis on his rank.

"Sorry, dear," Wayne apologized, sounding completely insincere. He smirked in John's direction. "I love it when she gets military on me."

They pulled up to the front of the restaurant and the kids tumbled out of the door, with Linda close on their heels. Wayne retrieved Jenny's crutches from the rear of the van as John helped her from the back seat. He watched as she took a moment to find her footing. When he reached out to steady her, his forearm inadvertently brushed against her breast. A fleeting collision with warmth and softness before she flinched away.

John could feel color rising up his neck. Every muscle in his body seemed to lock in place. He couldn't look at her, let her see the raging battle in his eyes. He had always prided himself on his ability to control his emotions. Until Jenny.

Each time he saw her he was bombarded with the need to watch her, to touch her, to taste her. And now one innocent, accidental touch had overrun his defenses. He was swamped by the same erotic sensations he'd experienced while reading her letters.

Feeling like a sex-starved ogre, John drew in a deep breath. Jenny was hurt and vulnerable and very determined not to get involved. How could he, of all people, forget that fact? He wasn't interested in a relationship, either, and he'd promised not to push. If he could only convince his body to have a conscience.

Frowning, John watched Jenny maneuver the crutches into the proper position. She kept her face perfectly blank, like someone who'd had a lot of practice at hiding pain.

He remembered times when Kenny had tried to hide his pain. Times John had had to leave the room when the doctors or nurses had come in to work on him. It was either leave or start punching someone.

"Does it hurt much?"

Jenny glanced up with a halfhearted smile. "Only my ego." Her lips tightened as she stepped up onto the curb. "Well, maybe a little more than my ego."

Once they were seated, Jenny seemed to forget all about her ego. John watched her laugh and talk to the boys. She even returned some of Wayne's humorous gibes. It was the first time he had seen her completely relaxed. He could hardly take his eyes off her, her face . . . her mouth. This was the loving, sensual woman who'd written him letters, not the woman who bravely suffered through her pain and could barely walk.

I wanted to be kissed for the rest of the night, for the rest of my life . . .

Stop it, John! he ordered and made an effort to get his thoughts back on neutral ground. Then he realized everyone was staring at him.

"What?" he asked, nonplussed. He faced Wayne hoping the hungry look on his face would be attributed to the food.

"I said," Wayne reiterated with great emphasis, "have you decided what to do with the rest of your leave? R and R, you know?"

"Somewhere with a lot of water," John answered with a decided lack of enthusiasm. His eyes moved back to Jenny. Holding her attention, he mentally amended his list of places he'd like to play from the bed, couch and kitchen table...to a blanket on a beach. "But I have a few things to settle here first."

Jenny pinkened slightly. Her fingers twisted the piece of bread she was holding into two pieces. "What things, Captain?" Her voice was full of warning and challenge.

John couldn't resist the urge to tease her until she blushed again. She thought he wouldn't say it. She was wrong.

"You, for one," he replied.

Jenny's eyes widened for a second, then her gaze shifted toward the boys, who were busy drawing pictures on the paper place mats. When she met John's gaze again she was blushing furiously. "As soon as we get home, I'll be settled. There's no need for you to worry about me."

"Who's worried?" John impulsively wished the restaurant and all the people in it would vanish, leaving him alone with Jenny. He would tell her exactly what they needed to settle. His attention shifted to her mouth again. Maybe he'd even show her. A kiss couldn't hurt....

"Well." Wayne intervened. He glanced from his friend to his sister-in-law with unabashed interest.

John knew he'd done it now. He could practically hear the wheels clicking like tumblers in Wayne's devious mind.

"Isn't this a kick?" Wayne drawled. "You two need some time alone? The rest of us could move to another table."

"Wayne!" exclaimed both John and Jenny. The simultaneous outburst dissipated the tension and everyone laughed. John smiled into Jenny's beautiful blue eyes and felt as if he truly was home.

"HERE WE ARE, home at last," Linda announced, holding the front door of Jenny's house open so that she could get through.

Jenny wanted to dance and cry at the same time. Well, maybe not dance, she thought ruefully. But she was home. No more hospital, ever, if she could help it.

John followed her through the door carrying her flowers, her magic bag and the overnight bag Linda had brought to the hospital. She had mixed emotions about his presence in her house. She hadn't invited him, yet the situation didn't feel as awkward as she'd imagined. He'd seen her at her worst, flat on her back, unable to walk, and he seemed to have taken it in stride. She frowned at the unintentional pun. She needed to concentrate on getting better again, and she didn't want to worry about entertaining or encumbering John.

"Where do you want this?" he asked, scattering her thoughts as easily as he had outmaneuvered her resistance to his presence.

"The couch is fine," she answered.

He tossed the bags down and turned to her, his hands resting on his hips. The unrelenting severity of his uniform couldn't camouflage the charged emotions running beneath the surface. For the first time he looked unsure.

Wayne had remained outside with the children, waiting for John. Linda would be driving back after she got Jenny settled. As if she sensed their need for privacy, Linda moved toward the open door. "I'll just say goodbye to the boys," she called over her shoulder.

John watched Linda leave, then turned back to Jenny. "You'll be okay?" He surveyed the interior of the house, stopping at the staircase. "You don't have to get up those stairs, do you?"

Jenny balanced her full weight on the crutches as she faced him. She was suddenly tired. It had been a long day, but, more than that, her fear and confusion had returned. John was going, which was exactly what she wanted. She refused to need anyone again. So why did she wish he'd stay?

"I'll be fine," she answered, dredging up a smile. She made a vague motion with one hand toward two doorways to the right. "I sleep downstairs."

Obviously reassured by her answer, he centered his attention on her again. He took one step toward her, then another. Gazing up at him kept her from collapsing onto the couch.

"Will you call me later?" he asked, so near her now that she steadied herself not to flinch if he touched her. And he looked as if he was definitely going to touch her.

"Yes," she answered without argument. She would call him. She wanted to hear his voice, to know he was somewhere in the world thinking of her.

One of his large hands came up to cup her cheek. Heat seemed to shimmer under the weight of his palm, and her skin felt electric. She couldn't move, could hardly breathe.

His voice sounded rough and too close. "Jenny, I have to . . ." He frowned. "All day I've wanted to . . . Oh, the hell with it." He lowered his head until their breath mingled. "Welcome home, Jenny," he said in a whisper before his lips met hers.

Jenny arched her neck upward. For once she was glad of the awkward support of her crutches. Otherwise she would have thrown herself into his arms, or collapsed at his feet. One way or another, she would have made a fool of herself over a simple kiss.

There was nothing simple about this kiss, though. After the first sweet touch he slowly raised his lips from hers. His fingers gently tilted her mouth to a better position before he tasted her again, this time lingering, savoring.

Jenny felt his warmth spiraling downward through her body, moving under her skin like a drug. Pain seemed a distant memory.

She inhaled the clean, starchy smell of his uniform, the faint spiciness of after-shave, the moist warmth of his mouth. She moaned the sound of his name, ignoring the warnings shouting in her mind. She wanted more, more of him, more of this, and opened her lips to welcome the heat.

"Excuse me." Linda's voice echoed through Jenny's brain as if her sister were calling down a well. John relinquished her mouth. But he didn't move away.

Jenny looked up into eyes the color of pewter and saw what must be reflected in hers. Desire, charged and urgent, mixed with surprise. She hadn't expected a real kiss from him to be so much better than the ones she had imagined. Maybe he hadn't expected it, either. His hand tightened for an instant as if to punctuate the clear meaning in his gaze. Then his fingers shifted along her cheek, down to her neck, in a caress that set her teeth on edge. She swayed toward him, following his touch. His hands bracketed her shoulders to steady her.

"Call me," he said again, an almost gruff order, with eyes as serious as the unresolved situation between them. He squeezed her shoulders before stepping back. After nodding to Linda, he closed the door behind him as if he needed to put some kind of solid barrier between what he wanted—Jenny—and what he had to do—leave.

Jenny would have smiled if she hadn't been in the same state of mind. She felt like an observer, knowing the situation was getting way out of hand, like a loaded semi picking up speed as it rolled downhill. Heading for serious trouble. Delicious, scorching, but nonetheless *serious* trouble, and she had to be the one who found the brakes.

A wave of sadness overwhelmed her. There could be no future for them. As soon as he realized how incapacitated she was, as soon as he saw her scars, he would disappear so fast the magicians of the world would be jealous.

But when he'd kissed her she'd felt normal, desirable, willing. Beautiful. It would be difficult to give that up.

9

THIS IS NOT A GOOD IDEA, Jenny thought for the hundredth time. So why hadn't she said no when John had called? Because she hadn't seen him since Monday—two whole days ago? Because just the sound of the doorbell, signaling he was on the other side of the door, sent her heart racing?

Jenny made her way to the front door, alternately thinking of reasons to keep him at a distance and wondering whether her hair looked all right. He'd wanted to take her out to eat, but that seemed too much like a date. She'd come to regret that decision, though. At least it would have been neutral ground. Now she had to contend with his presence in her house, in her life, even if it was only for an evening.

"Hi," she said, swinging the door open, making a great effort to appear nonchalant. She'd missed him, more than she wanted to admit, more than she dared show. Although he was dressed in civilian clothes, his relaxed but correct stance and his buzz cut screamed the fact that he was, without a doubt, military. He faced the world like a person who knew exactly who he was and where he was going. So unlike herself, Jenny thought with a pang. Then he smiled and she lost track of thought in general.

"Did you order a pizza, lady? And a movie?" He held up a large box with two video cassette cases balanced on top.

She stifled the urge to laugh and throw her arms around him. Going along with the game was safer. "I wasn't aware that the military delivered pizzas...and movies," she replied, acting puzzled.

His smile warmed as he inspected her from head to foot. Jenny wondered if he guessed she was wearing new sweats for the occasion.

"You'd be amazed at how versatile the military can be with the right motivation."

As always, they seemed to be carrying on two conversations at once. His gray eyes danced with mischief as he waited for her reply. Jenny pulled her gaze away from his look of lecherous expectancy and gingerly moved out of his path. "Well, motivate yourself in this direction, Captain," she ordered. "I'm hungry."

Although the words were obviously not the ones he'd hoped to hear, he let it slide. He stepped past her and relegated the pizza box to the coffee table.

He held up the paper sack in his other hand. "I brought beer and a bottle of wine. What do you want?"

Jenny momentarily thought of Drew, of being careful. Walking under the influence might be as dangerous for her as driving. The lure of being normal, of sharing a glass of wine over a pizza with a man tugged at her. Well, she didn't have far to walk in any case. "Sure. Wine would be great," she answered, then frowned. So many simple things to remind her she wasn't whole. "You'll have to help me get the glass down." She started for the kitchen.

"All we need is a candle and we're in business." He followed her through the kitchen door. "Do you have one hidden away in here someplace?" He scanned his surroundings with the precision and interest of an advance scout.

"In the third drawer." Jenny watched him excavate the package of emergency candles from her tool drawer. Whether it was the military aura or simply the man, John's presence seemed to dominate the familiar angles of the kitchen, changing her image of it after all these years, cementing his place in her memories, in her life, in her house. Like a dozing sleepwalker, she suddenly snapped out of her reverie. She couldn't spend the evening staring at him. She stepped over to another drawer and rummaged around to find a corkscrew.

The next time she glanced up, she saw he was studying the two photos stuck to the refrigerator by a magnet shaped like a slice of watermelon.

She knew every centimeter of those pictures by heart. One was of Linda, Wayne and the boys. The other was a family portrait of a family that no longer existed. "That's my mom with Linda and me," she said, noticing which one had caught his attention. *With Wayne and Randy,* she added silently. "Mom died three years ago. This was her house . . . our house growing up, I mean." Jenny stumbled on. "I moved back when I got out of the hospital."

John turned to look at her, one hand still hovering near the edge of the photo. "And your dad? Where is he?"

"He died when I was nineteen."

"I'm sorry."

His gaze was so potent she experienced its compassion across three feet of empty air. "Thanks."

His eyes found the photo again. "You looked happy then."

She had been happy, hadn't she? The picture had been taken before Randy had made the pro soccer team, before he seemed to be gone more than he was home. To Jenny, the emotions of that particular moment had thinned and paled, as if a lifetime had passed between then and now.

"Is this your ex-husband?" John's terse question caught her by surprise. Were her thoughts written on her forehead?

"How did . . . Who told you I was married?"

"You did, *Mrs.* Teale," he answered matter-of-factly. "The first day I met you. And Linda told me about your ex-husband." His features had lost all warmth and playfulness. He pushed away from the refrigerator and its reminder of the past. Instead of looking at her, however, he reached up to pluck a wineglass from an overhead rack. "Sounds like he was a helluva guy."

"Was?" Jenny noticed he had spoken in the past tense. "He's still alive."

John faced her without flinching or smiling. "Too bad."

"I DON'T BELIEVE THIS." Jenny laughed as she opened the second movie case. "*Lethal Weapon* and *Delta Force?* Were they all out of real movies?"

John finished pouring the wine before looking at her with a grin. "Those are real movies."

"Sure, if you like to watch things blow up."

He deftly lifted the movie cassette out of her hand and sauntered over to the VCR. "Isn't it comforting to see how your tax dollars are supposed to work?" He cocked one eyebrow as he shoved the cassette into the machine. "And the good guys always win."

The good guys, Jenny repeated silently. John was definitely one of those, but that didn't make him any less dangerous to her peace of mind.

The movie title lit the screen as John sat next to her. He braced his arm along the sofa back as his gaze swept over her. "So, how have you been?"

"Better," Jenny managed to say without squirming under his perusal. Her left hand automatically kneaded her damaged thigh. "I still have a nice bruise." John was staring at the movement of her hand. She stopped. "It's healing."

"Well, you should get comfortable." Without any warning he bent, grasped her calves with his hands and carefully lifted her legs into his lap. "Is that all right?" He ignored the startled look on Jenny's face as he peeled back the velcro fasteners of her shoes and tossed one, then the other, to the floor.

Jenny was used to being handled by Drew. John was a different story altogether. When he touched her, she never thought of pain, only pleasure. And heat. He settled her calves across his thighs as if that was where they belonged, and she felt scorched. Before she could react properly, or even improperly, he handed her a glass of wine, then picked up his bottle of beer. "To feeling better."

Muted gunfire served as background noise while they ate. John made Jenny smile by citing several examples of movies that proved Hollywood didn't know a thing about how the military really worked. They had made a serious dent in the pizza and John was pouring Jenny her second glass of wine when he asked about the accident.

Relaxed and off guard, Jenny didn't hesitate; it felt right to tell him. "It's funny," she said, "how a few seconds can change an entire life. Before that day I would have qualified for a show called 'The Normal and Boring.'" She met his eyes as she accepted the wineglass. "I don't mean that everything was perfect. My marriage..." An agonizing wave of embarrassment swamped her. How could she explain failure to this man? By claiming it was bad luck? She anchored her gaze on the glass, but her sight was filled with the past, with Randy and the struggle to understand him. "When I look back, I realize that, for the most part, I was naive. I thought things would work out. I was waiting for the fairy tale, for the happily-ever-after part." A husband who loved her, who was faithful, and a family...

"And now you have life all figured out," John chided.

"No." With a shaking hand she ran a finger along the rim of the glass. Now her life had been rearranged with fewer choices. She didn't have to concern herself with decisions like which man she ought to marry, how long to wait before having children, or how many to have.... She wouldn't be having any. "No, I don't have life figured out," she said. "But my expectations are different."

"Such as?"

Did he really want to hear the truth? she wondered as she met his eyes once more. She stared at him for a long moment. Like it or not, he needed to know. "Such as, we can only depend on ourselves. And happily ever after doesn't exist."

John looked as if he wanted to interrupt.

"We all have to face the fact that ultimately we are alone in the world. Promises and vows don't change that," she insisted.

"You *want* to be alone?" His voice sounded incredulous, almost angry.

"What I want or wanted had little to do with it."

"I'm talking about now, for the remainder of your life." In an abrupt movement he set his beer bottle on the table with enough force to betray his anger. "Because one man wimped out on you, you're giving up on all the rest?" With care that belied his agitated state, he lifted her legs and got to his feet. The movie had ended. John paced to the VCR as if he needed to do something—anything.

Jenny found herself speaking to his back. "It's not just men." She could feel her throat tightening with old pain. She shouldn't have had the wine. It was making this so much more difficult to explain. "Soon I'll have enough money from the insurance settlement so that I can move and won't have to depend on anybody for anything." She'd been abandoned by a husband and lost her child. "I don't *want* to feel that way again."

John pivoted to face her the moment she mentioned money. In a few short seconds he was standing over her. "Liar."

Jenny stared up at him, feeling the first stirring of her own anger. Why couldn't he accept her point of view? Why couldn't he see that this was something she had to do to survive? She couldn't handle any more tragedy, any more emotional storms.

He dropped beside her on the couch, sitting hip-to-hip, trapping her in the cage of his arms. He was barely touching her, but he was too close, the intense look in his gray eyes too demanding. Jenny's anger changed to wariness.

"Money can't buy everything." He stared into her eyes like a mind reader searching for a glimpse of the future. "People need each other." His fingers grazed her cheek before pushing into her hair. "Your letters were full of that longing, of that wanting," he accused in a taut voice. He lowered his head until Jenny felt the brush of his breath on her lips. "Is this what you're afraid of feeling? Afraid of needing?" He kissed her cheek, her chin and, for a long and languorous moment, her lips.

She didn't resist, but she didn't participate, either. Even as her body was shifting minutely, accommodating itself to the shape of him, the feel of him, her brain was sorting through responses at a speed just short of overload. The pounding of her heart, pumping heat through her veins like a scalding surge, echoed in her ears.

John pulled back slightly and drew in a deep, satisfied breath. If he'd been angry, he didn't seem to be any longer. His mouth was so close she felt him smile before he spoke, teasing her lips with his words. "What's the matter, Jenny? Are you afraid to kiss me back?"

Startled by how much she suddenly wanted to kiss him, she feebly tried to push him away. "John—"

"Kiss me. Just once really kiss me—like you wanted to be kissed in the letters."

Her body responded to his voice, to the barely concealed ache in the sound, not the words or their meaning. The fingers of her left hand grasped the folds of his shirt as her mouth found his. Expecting a sweet, teasing ripple of passion, Jenny was bowled over by a tidal flood. She gave herself up to the skimming weightlessness of total awareness, of total surrender. His lips pressed hers open, claiming, readying her mouth for his tongue. Then, after winding through her passion-drugged senses, the words he'd spoken penetrated Jenny's soaring mind.

The letters.

One of his hands slipped behind her, to the small of her back, and lifted her closer. Jenny shuddered, feeling as if she had slipped through a patch of thin ice into frigid water. The involuntary flinch sent a spasm of pain down her leg. She gasped and pushed out of the embrace.

He let go immediately, a frown of concern on his face. His hands ran up her arms in a soothing motion. "I hurt you. I'm—"

"The letters weren't real!" Jenny retreated until no part of her body was touching his and pinned him with an accusing look. She shoved one hand through her hair and swallowed against the insistent itch of gathering tears. "You said you wanted to be my friend, but you're looking for the woman in the letters. The fantasy." Disappointment and chagrin dragged at her like gravity. He didn't care about her; he was simply turned on by her letters. She forced herself to hold his serious gray gaze. "That woman doesn't exist. I made her up. Do you hear me?"

"No, Jenny." His fingers brushed the hair near her ear, trying to calm her. She flinched, but he continued. "Listen to me for a second."

Even though her body was stiff and unyielding, he had her attention. "Part of that's true. I remember more than I should about those letters. And I won't lie and say they didn't affect me. But I meant it when I said I wanted to be your friend." He sighed. "I know you made up the letters. I don't expect anything because of them.

"Some of the game was real, though. The caring and the hope were real. And the wanting. You might not want—" he hesitated slightly "—want me, but it doesn't make those feelings less valid."

"This has nothing to do with you," she snapped in exasperation.

"I hope you're wrong. I hope it has everything to do with me." He smiled a cheerless smile. "But even if it doesn't, I still want to be the one to prove it to you." The smile wavered. "I did push and I'm sorry. I'm just so damned—" He looked into her eyes, then his gaze dropped to her mouth. He seemed to lose track of the point he'd started to make. "I got a little carried away."

Carried away was not how Jenny would describe what had happened to her. Blown away was more like it. She watched him like a shock victim, fighting the effects of his nearness, the afterburn of his kiss.

John witnessed the war of emotion in her blue eyes and experienced the unsettling realization that he had grabbed hold of an emotional rip cord. One moment he was free-falling, slicing through the air like a diving hawk, enjoying the rush. The next he was yanked upward, forcibly reminded that he was out of control.

Pull yourself together, John, he ordered silently. He was a grown man, a man who prided himself on logic and control. So why did this one woman make him forget all of that? She'd responded to the kiss. He had felt it, tasted it. Why was she fighting so hard to keep him at a distance?

Why was he fighting so hard to get closer? That distracting question stopped him. Why did it bother him to hear her talk about moving away and about having all the money she needed to take care of herself?

Mentally he took a step backward and latched on to the first available answer. Because he wanted to help. He was doing it for her, to show her she was still alive, still desirable, and that she still needed someone in her life.

He simply didn't intend to make a career out of it.

"Look," he said, raising his hands in surrender. "From now on I promise not to push. No touching...." His gaze brushed her mouth again. "No kissing. Okay?"

It seemed to take a long time before she nodded in agreement.

"But you have to promise something, too." She looked wary again, and John fought the urge to reach out to her.

"If a time comes when you want me to touch you, or to kiss you, you have to tell me. Will you do that?" He couldn't resist an impertinent grin. "All you have to do is ask."

John,
Today was such an odd day. Life goes on minute by minute, hour by hour, and I'm grateful. For as time passes, it brings us closer to the moment when we'll be together. All I can think of is how much I want you to hold me, to touch me, and yet today the simple joy of being alive and the anticipation of a bright future have been my inspiration.

Our future. I have started planning for the day you come home. I put new curtains up in our bedroom. Bought new sheets, new pillows and, more importantly, something to wear that I can only describe as silky and sexy and very, very short. The saleswoman said the color complements the color of my eyes. Not that I expect to wear it long enough for you to notice. Please have your blood pressure checked before you board the flight home. I'll handle the endurance test.

I intend to make you a very happy man.

Jenny

JOHN FOLDED THE LETTER and stuffed it back into the matching blue envelope. He'd planned to sit calmly and study Jenny's letters, then figure out how to use them to convince her she needed and wanted someone. But there was no way to be calm as he reread her words.

Not now. Not after meeting her, after kissing her. His imagination was fueled by too much real information. He knew how she pushed her fingers through her feathery blond hair when she was nervous. He knew how the corners of her lips turned up even when she was trying not to smile. He knew how those lips tasted. . . .

He knew where she lived.

John pushed the envelope back into the box with the others and stood. It took a moment or two for him to find his keys. He had to go somewhere. He couldn't just sit and imagine. He needed noise and conversation. He needed a beer, and there was a whole list of his buddies who'd be willing to buy.

"I NEED A WOMAN. Any woman," John announced to the table in general as the waitress retreated from sight. There was a heartbeat of silence before the three men seated with him burst into whoops of laughter.

"You?" First Lieutenant Everett Hardin nearly choked on his first sip of beer. "Since when do you need advice on where to find women? Don't they always fall out of the sky and into your lap?" He set his glass down and smirked at Captain Putnam sitting to his right. "Do you know what happened to this lucky SOB at the Fourth of July parade last year?"

Putnam leaned forward as John tucked in his chin and paid an inordinate amount of attention to his glass of beer.

"Braithwaite was standing next to the—what was it?— the History of Kansas Cowgirls float?" He went on without an answer. "Anyway, old John here was talking to a couple of the organizers when one of the cowgirls took a wrong step off the edge of the float." Lieutenant Hardin could hardly finish the story, he was laughing so hard. "So what do you think? Does she break her neck, or her leg, or even get a run in her panty hose? No, not with Captain John around. Can you believe it?" he asked as he held his arms like a cradle. "He catches her."

Hardin reached over and playfully punched John on the shoulder. "She falls right into his arms." He took a pull of beer then added slyly, "We didn't see either one of them for the rest of the weekend." All the men at the table laughed.

"Something that happened a year ago doesn't do me much good tonight," John said, refusing to deny the story. He absently scanned the nearly empty bar. He needed a woman, tonight, and all he could think about was Jenny. Somehow, some way, she'd infiltrated his dreams, his fantasies. By the second letter she'd become his type. And by the time he'd met her at the homecoming celebration, she'd become his obsession.

"Hey, do you remember Sherry Howard? I saw her over in Aggieville the other night." A calculating smile moved across the lieutenant's face. "She looked available."

John brought his mind back to the conversation. He took a swallow of beer. "Didn't she used to go around with what's-his-name?"

"Lyles."

"Yeah." John frowned. "I hate that guy."

"Well, sure, but Sherry—"

John held up a hand to halt the conversation. "Definitely a woman with poor judgment. I'll pass." He was beginning to worry about his own judgment. He had promised Jenny no pressure. What a stupid thing to promise. And he knew Darla would be pleased to hear from him again, so why was he sitting in a bar complaining? He flexed his jaw in frustration. Just because the thought of Jenny, the remembered taste of her made his body go hot and tight?

"I thought you said any woman," Putnam prodded.

John shrugged, then glanced toward the pay telephone on the far wall. He'd forgotten Darla's number. He'd have to look it up. But he made no move toward the phone. He was beginning to realize that after meeting Jenny, no other woman would do.

"Ahh, here comes one now." Hardin grinned before turning to watch the approach of the cocktail waitress. She was dressed in shorts with an oversize T-shirt and looked more like a college student than a barmaid. She stopped with a glance toward their glasses.

"Need anything?"

Lieutenant Hardin grabbed her left hand with both of his. "Will you marry me and bear my children?" he pleaded.

She gave him a deadpan stare. "No."

He managed to look hurt, then hopeful. "I suppose a few hours of meaningless sex is out of the question, then?"

With a sigh the waitress jerked her hand free and rolled her eyes skyward before walking away.

"Thanks a lot, Hardin," Putnam said, looking put out. "I wanted another beer."

THIS WAS TOO MUCH to expect from a mortal man, John fumed as he parked his truck in the hospital parking lot the next afternoon. Why should he drive himself crazy trying to help Jenny? Trying to convince her of anything? If he was going to break all his rules and get involved with a woman, he wanted one who was warm and willing—a woman who would meet him halfway, not one he had to worry about and watch as she suffered. He should just walk away. He should throw out her letters and forget her blue eyes and . . .

All right, so he was obsessed. It could be worse. After a restless, nearly sleepless night—spent alone—John had decided on the first step of a plan, and after lunch he'd set it in motion.

He pushed the button for the elevator, then nervously shoved his hands into his pockets. He would never feel comfortable inside the walls of a hospital. One more reason he should be running in the other direction from Jenny.

The elevator doors opened. John stared at the empty car for a second, then stepped inside. He had gone over this meeting in his mind at least fifty times. He knew exactly what he wanted to say, what he wanted to know. It was the outcome he was worried about. By asking questions, he'd be forced to hear answers. Some of those answers could be worse than the agony of not knowing.

"What does remission mean?" The sudden memory rocked him back on his heels. *"Well,"* the doctor had answered. *"It means with a little bit of luck, your brother will get better."*

A little bit of luck, John thought ruefully. Two months later his brother had died. Grief and guilt flared behind John's grown-up logic. He knew he couldn't have saved his brother, but he still wished he could have given him that little bit of luck.

John found Drew's office without any problem. He faced a door that stood half-open. The wall next to it was covered with photographs and newspaper clippings. Most of the clippings had headings like Teenager, Feared Paralyzed After Fall From Roof, Takes First Steps. John scanned the wall searching for an all-too-familiar face.

He found Jenny's picture near the top. She looked so frail, standing with the help of two crutches. Yet she was smiling and holding up one of her strange-looking pup-

pets. After sucking in a back-stiffening breath and reminding himself he was doing this for her, he knocked
near a cartoon sign that read The Doktor Is IN.

"Well, hello, Captain. This must be Jenny Teale Day."
Drew looked surprised and almost wary to see him.

"Is today her day for therapy?" John asked as he shook
the therapist's hand.

"Yes, she was here earlier." Drew's eyes met his steadily. "But I get the feeling you already knew that." Shifting into a businesslike manner, Drew scooped some
charts out of a chair and angled it closer to his desk. "Sit
down. What can I do for you?"

No use avoiding the issue, John decided. "I want to ask
you about Jenny, about how she's doing."

Drew leaned back in his chair and crossed his arms
over his thick chest, a defensive and somewhat forbid-
ding gesture. "How she's doing, huh? You're the second
person today to ask me about her, and I have to tell you
the same thing the other person was told. I can't discuss
my patients."

The second person? John refused to be diverted, even
though his plan seemed to be disintegrating before his
eyes. "I need to know about her strength, her physical
limitations."

"You'll need to ask her."

"I can't ask her, she— Damn." John ran a hand over
his face. Time for plan B. Trouble was, he didn't have one
yet.

Drew watched John for what seemed like an eternity
before he spoke. "You know, I really would like to help
you out, since you're a friend of Jenny's. But legally and
ethically I can't talk about *her* medical history." The
therapist stared at John intently. "Now, if you stopped
in here for some advice about a hypothetical friend who

might be facing similar medical problems, that would be a different story."

John didn't have to be hit by a truck to get the picture. He scrambled for words. "Right. Say I had this friend who was in an accident a while—over a year ago. And she's worked hard to get well but she's still on crutches. . . ."

"You want to know if this friend will be able to walk without crutches? Will she dance, play softball?"

"No." John hoped his face wasn't the dull red color he thought it was. He hadn't blushed since he was twelve. He shifted in the chair, trying to find a more comfortable position. "I mean, I figure if she's been able to get this far, she'll be able to walk all right someday." He cleared his throat and stared at the other man, wishing Drew could read his mind for the next few seconds so he wouldn't have to say the words. "I need to know how strong she is . . . might be now. If it would hurt her to . . . if I would hurt her if I . . ." The image of Jenny naked in his arms, moving beneath him in shared pleasure, obliterated his rehearsed speech. John took a deep breath and plunged ahead. "I'm talking about sex."

Drew's features remained impassive. John decided this was not a man who would be thrown off kilter by any question. He should be in the precinct or the priesthood.

"Let me get this straight," Drew said carefully. "You don't want to know if your friend will walk without a limp or if she can keep up with your long, normal legs? You just want to know if it would hurt her to have sex? Now, while she's still on crutches?"

"That's the question."

Drew uncrossed his arms and looked as if he would like to shake John's hand again. This time with more enthusiasm. "What did *this friend* say?"

The ability to explain what was happening between him and Jenny eluded John. He couldn't explain it to himself. He knew he was completely fascinated by her strength and worried by her weakness. He wanted to touch her, hold her, taste her with an urgency. When they were together she seemed to mirror his desires. He knew he made her nervous, and he accepted that as a good sign.

When he had touched her, kissed her, her mouth and body responded to his with a yes, but he knew if he voiced the question, the answer would be no. That's why he'd asked Drew first, so that he would know how far he should go to persuade her mind of what her body wanted. Of what his body craved.

"I haven't asked her," John managed to say, pushing past the erotic images flooding his mind. "I plan to convince her."

The big Irishman smiled. "Normal, missionary sex— nothing kinky, no hanging from chandeliers?"

"Whatever works." *A bed, a couch, the rug...*

Drew's eyes twinkled. "In my professional opinion, there is, most likely, no physical reason why she couldn't. Assuming, of course, that you're a patient and even-handed guy. Pay attention. You'll know if you're hurting her."

The weight of uncertainty lifted from John's mind. This was a battle he could fight. Jenny was getting better and better every day—not like his brother. Now all he had to do was convince her. To prove to her she was the woman in the letters, in the dreams. He moved to the edge of his chair, ready to leave. "Listen, I— Thanks," he said as he stood.

"Hey, don't thank me yet." Drew had lost his humorous mood as he stood, too. Instead of saying goodbye he hesitated, making some sort of silent decision.

John waited.

"It shouldn't hurt for you and your friend to make love if you're both agreeable. In fact, it might actually help her attitude." Drew reluctantly added, "But, I have to say, it might hurt you."

"What do you mean?" John asked, perplexed. He was healthy as the proverbial horse. He'd just had a physical evaluation on his return from the Middle East.

Drew cleared his throat, looking as uncomfortable as John had only a few short moments before. He also appeared aggravated.

"Well," he said, meeting John's gaze with serious eyes. "The other person asking about Jenny today was a man."

John knew bad news when it was being delivered, yet he felt too relieved about Jenny to worry. He was busy planning the next part of the campaign.

"This man said he was her husband."

John's plans came to a sudden, screeching halt. "Her *ex*-husband," he corrected tautly, but even as he said it, he felt uneasy.

10

"TAKE A RIDE WITH ME."

Jenny balanced on her crutches and self-consciously glanced down at her baggy sweats and old tennis shoes. "But I—"

"Please."

John's gaze held hers, so steady, so serious she couldn't find the words to refuse. A tremor of worry surged through her. "Are you all right?"

"I've been better." He held out his hand. Without any thought about touching or trusting, she slipped her fingers into his. His grip tightened for a moment, then he let go and stepped out of her way. They were halfway through the door when Jenny's logic returned. She stopped. "I've got to get my keys and my purse."

John did an about-face. "Where are they?"

"On the table near the couch."

Minutes later he draped the strap of her purse over her shoulder. He followed her through the door, locked it and dropped the keys into her bag.

"Where are we going?" she asked, unable to keep the breathless sound out of her voice. He wasn't physically dragging her along but she felt like Dorothy, caught up in a relentless wind.

"I thought I'd give you a tour of the post," he said as he helped her into the passenger side of his truck. "Show you where I work." He didn't look at her as he spoke, and he closed the door firmly before she could answer.

Jenny was completely confounded. Fort Riley was almost an hour's drive away. He'd shown up at her door all grim and determined simply to take her on a tour of Fort Riley?

"John?" Jenny ventured as he backed the truck out of her driveway. "What's wrong?"

He focused an excessive amount of attention on his driving. He checked the mirrors, adjusted the fan of the air-conditioning. Finally he glanced at her. "I thought you needed to get out of that house, so I—"

"You're acting like the world is about to end."

Maybe it is, he thought. Too soon. He hadn't had time to convince her of anything, much less get past the barriers she'd built between herself and the world. Now the ex-husband was part of the equation.

He shrugged, feigning indifference. "Had a tough day, that's all."

"You could have at least let me change clothes," she chided.

Baffled by her words, he checked her out from her shoes to her hair. "You look fine. What's the problem?"

Jenny put a hand over her eyes and groaned. "These are my rattiest sweats. I wear them to clean house. I'm not getting out of this truck."

"Fine," he said. "We'll hit the drive-through at a hamburger joint in Junction City for dinner, then."

She groaned again. *Men!*

JENNY HAD BEEN to Fort Riley before to visit Linda and Wayne when they lived in base housing. But somehow it was different now, seeing it with John. This was the place he worked, where he spent the major portion of his time, and she wanted to know everything. He seemed to be in the mood to show her everything, too, from Mar-

shall Field to Custer Hill, from hundred-year-old lime-
stone buildings surrounded by huge trees to offices built
in the glass-and-block style of the fifties on hills without
a tree in the vicinity. Finally he pulled into a parking place
near one of the newer one-story buildings.

He took the truck out of gear and left the engine running. "This is where I work—" he smiled "—in case you
ever need to find me."

Jenny ignored the emphasis he put on the word need.
"Are you serious?" She swiveled in the seat to read the
street sign. "After all the turns we made I could never find
this place again."

"You want to go in?" His look was a dare.

"No." She softened the answer with a sheepish shrug.
"Not today, anyway. Can we make it another time?"

"Sure." He seemed happier with her answer than he
should have been. He shifted the truck into reverse and
backed out. "I spend too damned much time here as it is.
I'd rather show you where I live."

"Where you live?" Jenny swallowed and braced herself as he turned the corner at the end of the street.

On the fifteen-minute drive from Fort Riley to Manhattan, John remained in tour mode, detailing everything from the fire station to the local speed trap, as if he
was in real estate and she was thinking of relocating.
They hit the business areas in Manhattan and traffic increased, slowing their progress past a shopping mall.
Then they moved into the residential section where he
turned left into a U-shaped complex called Grayson Place
and pointed out his apartment on the lower level of a
tree-shaded row, second from the end.

He pulled into a parking space and shut off the truck's
engine, then opened his door. On the way around the
back of the truck he retrieved her crutches from the truck

bed. He opened her door and once more held out his hand to her. This time she didn't take it.

"John, I don't think..." Jenny's eyes skittered along the sidewalk to the windows facing the parking lot, feeling as though three hundred people were watching them.

"The apartments all look the same, but you may as well see the inside." His hand remained extended.

Jenny hesitated, unsure. Not afraid, exactly, just wary of the situation. Alone together in his apartment seemed much more suggestive than inviting him to her house for pizza. "But why—"

"Are you afraid of me?" He dropped his hand and stared into her eyes, waiting, no, *demanding* an answer. He seemed on the verge of giving her a piece of his mind.

"No. I'm not afraid of you." It was the two of them together, alone, that scared her spitless. Part of that—maybe three-quarters—had to do with the way her body responded to him, to a simple touch or... kiss. Her gaze traced the shape of his mouth before rising to meet his stare. There it was, the other quarter—his unerring determination. Simply speaking, every time he looked at her, his resolute gray eyes made it clear that once he made up his mind about something, he never gave up. If he decided on her...

He reached across and unfastened her seat belt. "Come on, then." He slid his hands around her waist to help her step down from the truck, and she didn't resist. For a moment they stood face-to-face, close enough for their clothes to touch. A slow somersault of awareness tumbled through Jenny's chest. She couldn't back away. Part of her didn't want to. Involuntarily her fingers tightened on his arms. Her touch seemed to jolt him into motion. He drew in a breath before he broke contact to hand her the crutches.

As John opened the door of his apartment and waited for Jenny to precede him, he had no doubts or illusions about why he'd brought her here. This apartment didn't mean a damn thing to him, until now, until Jenny walked through the door.

Then a flash of black came streaking toward them, nearly knocking her to the ground. John had forgotten about the dog. With unexpected zealousness the usually well-behaved Deeno planted his feet somewhere in the vicinity of her stomach.

"Get down, Deeno!" John ordered as he braced Jenny from behind. Unrepentant but obedient, the dog retreated, wagging his tail all the way. Worried, John brought one arm around her to help adjust her crutch. "Sorry. Are you okay?"

Jenny burst out laughing and, seeming to forget herself, leaned against him. "I guess you have a dog."

"He's a loaner. Belongs to a buddy of mine who's on temporary duty," John grumbled. "And the way the dog's going, he's not gonna survive the week." The sweet smell of Jenny's hair drifted upward, and he could feel the contours of her back along his chest. As a gentleman he should move away and help her get settled, but as a man he would stand there into the next century, or for as long as she wanted to lean on him.

Jenny caught her breath and began to recover. Maneuvering her crutches, she straightened her stance.

"Are you sure you're all right?" John asked as he placed himself between Jenny and the dog.

"I'm fine. He startled me, that's all"

"You want to sit down?" *Make it normal,* his mind ordered. "Want something to drink?" He walked into the small kitchen area with Deeno at his heels and opened the refrigerator. "I have soda or beer."

Peripherally he watched Jenny turn a complete circle in the living room before moving to stand beside him. Deeno sniffed her hand, then gave her knuckles a swipe with his tongue. Using her crutches for balance, she absently petted the dog as she peered over his arm to look into the refrigerator. "You're not kidding, are you?" She gestured toward the nearly empty shelves. "Soda and beer is *all* you have. Don't you ever cook?"

He shrugged before grabbing one soda and one beer, effectively making the decision for her. "I know how to cook," he answered a little defensively. "It's just easier and faster to eat out." With a smile he closed the door. "No dishes to wash." He held up the can. "Want a glass?"

She gave him a look that said she thought he might make her wash the glass after she was finished. "No, the can is fine."

John clamped one hand on Deeno's collar as Jenny headed for the end of the couch. She stopped before she reached it and looked down at a pair of scuffed-up running shoes abandoned near a chair.

"You're a runner." She didn't smile or frown, she simply made the statement.

He shrugged. "Yeah. Well, I ran track in college for a while." He shooed the dog to his favorite corner of the room and ordered him to lie down before he continued. "Now I train most mornings. But I still like to run in the afternoons." John glanced at his discarded shoes. He wished he'd kicked the damn things off and thrown them into the closet, out of sight. They seemed to glare like a neon sign: *I can run and you can't.* He thought of how he'd feel if he could never run again.

"Don't you want the rest of the tour?" He waved her toward the hallway, toward a different topic of conversation. She followed reluctantly.

"I thought women liked to check the bathroom for extra toothbrushes." He stopped in front of the open bedroom door. "Or the bedroom for damaging evidence, like a stray pair of ladies' panties." He braced an arm on the door frame, determined to look completely harmless, and gazed at her for a long minute. He wanted her undivided attention. "You've never asked me if I'm involved with a woman."

She blinked once, then looked past him to the neatly made bed before returning her gaze to him.

"I, uh—" She coughed. "I assumed you weren't, since . . ."

"I'm not." He dropped his arm and leaned his back against the wall before taking a sip of beer. His lips twisted into a wry smile as he swallowed. "It would have been nice if you'd wondered, though."

"I did wonder," she confessed breathlessly. "When I was writing to you, I . . ." The sentence trailed away; apparently she was uncomfortable talking about the letters.

In the letters *she* had been his woman. What would she think if he dug them out of the box and showed them to her? Showed her that her words meant enough for him to keep them, enough for him to want more. . . . His thoughts caused his voice to sound more abrupt than he intended.

"I've never had that irresistible urge to get married." He almost said, until now. Was he losing his mind? *Get a grip, John*, he fumed. He moved past her, then waited for her to follow him back to the living room, back to safe, neutral territory. Her silence seemed to be charged with unasked questions. He clenched his teeth and tried to get the conversation back to even ground. "I suppose I've had what you could call 'relationships.'"

When she was settled in a chair, John handed her the soda and kicked his running shoes out of sight before taking a seat on the couch. He concentrated on nonchalantly propping his feet on the coffee table next to his beer. "I've been too busy with my career to worry about finding a wife or having a family."

"So, you like being single?" Both her hands were wrapped around the soft drink can as if to prevent its escape. Deeno sauntered over and dropped his head on her thigh, begging for attention. One hand loosened from the can and stroked the dog's head.

John scrutinized her slender fingers as they moved slowly over the dog's black fur. He had to clear his throat before answering. "Not particularly." Not anymore, although he wasn't sure what he wanted to do about it. He'd lived for so long with his defenses up against personal involvement that he didn't know how to surrender. His mind answered by presenting a vivid image of the homecoming celebration. Only this time Jenny was smiling, waiting to welcome him, with his child in her arms. "I would like to be married, but only for the right reasons and to the right woman." He watched her assimilate his words, wondering what she was thinking.

"How about you? Do you miss having a husband? Don't you want to have kids?" As soon as the question was out of his mouth he regretted the words. She closed up faster than a night blooming flower caught by the sunshine.

"We talked about that before," she said, pronouncing the subject settled and closed.

"Okay." He grinned and raised his hands in surrender, forced to avoid that mine field for now. "What do you think of my apartment, then?"

Jenny looked surprised, then her lips curved into a fragile smile before she glanced around the room one more time. Deeno's head slid off her leg as he flopped down at her feet. "It could use some more furniture and maybe new curtains."

"What's wrong with the curtains?" John countered. "They open, they close."

"They're beige. I would buy—"

He watched her eyes widen slightly as she stopped.

I put new curtains up in our bedroom....

Deciding to rescue her, he said, "You mean they're supposed to look good?"

She nodded.

He studied the curtains for a moment, then shook his head. "In that case I guess I'll have to burn 'em."

Jenny laughed. John decided he could get used to the sound of her laughter. And the sight of it. Her natural, shadowless smile made something in his chest go haywire. Rather than sit there and stare at her, he pushed to his feet and held out his hand for her empty soda can. "Come on, I promised you a hamburger to go—"

The beeper on his belt went off. Deeno leaped to his feet and scrambled to the door as if the apartment were on fire. Immediately John switched it off. "Hang on a second," he said to Jenny. He tossed the can and beer bottle into the trash and headed for the phone.

"What's up?"

Jenny listened to the one-sided conversation, amazed at the change that came over John. His whole demeanor, even the timbre of his voice, shifted into that of a commander.

"Have you tried to find him?" John looked at his watch and frowned. He listened for a few moments. "All right." He picked up a pen. "Where are his quarters?"

"ONE OF MY MEN DIDN'T make formation," John explained as he ushered her out of his apartment. "He's got some kind of problem at home." He opened the truck door and relieved her of her crutches as she got in. "I need to stop by there and find out what's going on before I take you back."

Again, Jenny desperately wished she'd changed clothes before they left. John slid into the driver's seat and glanced in her direction.

"What's wrong?"

"Nothing. I, uh, I can wait in the truck while you do this, right?"

John frowned and started the truck's engine. "Yeah, no problem."

They traveled the short distance to Fort Riley and in a few minutes were pulling in to the parking lot of the enlisted men's housing area. This was basic army issue—a row of boxlike apartments, each exactly the same as the next.

The first thing Jenny noticed was that every modest yard seemed to have one or two children in it.

John parked the truck in an area across from a small play area. The grass—or at least, what hadn't been pulverized by tiny feet—was trimmed neatly around the swing set and the teeter-totter. Jenny's eyes were drawn to two little girls, three or four, playing in the sand near the slide.

"This should only take a few minutes," John said as he stepped out of the truck. He had on what Jenny could only describe as his stern captain's face, and she had to smile. It seemed somebody was in trouble.

"I'll be fine. Take your time."

With a nod he walked away. She watched him cross the grass in a few long strides and knock on one of the doors.

In less than a moment the door was opened by an impossibly young-looking soldier. Jenny could hear a baby crying inside, but then John disappeared over the threshold and the door closed behind him.

Closer to the truck, another child let out a yelp and started to cry. Jenny turned her eyes back to the playground in time to see a young mother pick up her son from the ground and dust him off. A shaft of pain went through Jenny as she watched the woman set the child back on his feet before laughingly chasing him around the slide—such an ordinary action. Something Jenny would never be able to do.

John's voice interrupted the downward spiral of her thoughts. Jenny swiveled in the seat toward the sound. He and the young soldier were standing on the threshold of the apartment. The soldier was rocking the wailing baby now while another child pulled on the leg of his uniform with its small arms raised. The soldier's wife stood in the doorway and appeared ready to cry, too. Jenny could see John gesture and point to his watch, but she couldn't hear the words. Suddenly, without breaking concentration, John bent and scooped up the whining child at their feet, balancing him in the crook of his arm. Immediately contented, the child stuck one thumb in his mouth and tugged on John's collar with the other hand.

Jenny's heart seemed to swell and fill, as if it might burst. John would make such a good father. Why hadn't he married and had his own children? Why did he spend all of his time taking care of everyone else?

The baby hiccuped and stopped crying, so that Jenny could hear them.

"Follow me over there now," John insisted. "We only have a few minutes before the office closes."

"Yes, sir," was the young man's only reply.

John set down the child he was holding and aimed him toward his mother with a light pat on his backside. A moment later he slid into the truck and started it in one smooth motion. He fastened his seat belt single-handedly as he backed out of the space. "One more stop."

At that instant Jenny could only hope that her voice would be steady. "Where's that?" she managed to say.

"The office of the power company. Their power's been cut off."

As they drove through the parking lot, Jenny got one more glimpse of the soldier's wife, standing in the open doorway, rocking the baby.

"Will they be able to get it fixed today?" she asked.

John appeared to be distinctly annoyed. "It doesn't have to be fixed," he said in a tight voice. "It has to be paid."

"He doesn't have any money? Then how—"

"Let's put it this way," John cut in as he made a quick left turn that pressed Jenny against the door. "Today Private Williams's captain is putting down a hundred bucks toward that bill. Tomorrow . . ." John smiled like a man who thoroughly enjoyed his work. "Like it or not, Private Williams is going to learn more about budgeting than he *ever* wanted to know."

11

"WHY DON'T YOU COME OVER for dinner tomorrow night?" Linda asked Jenny. "Just a second. Let your brother have it, Tee. There's another one in the refrigerator." The phone clanked against something. "Sorry. Anyway, you've been barricaded in that house long enough, and we're having sort of a celebration."

"Oh? What are you celebrating?"

"Well, it's supposed to be a surprise but I don't want to spring it on you without warning." Linda was silent for a brief instant. "I'm pretty sure I'm pregnant again."

Jenny couldn't speak as words from the past intruded on her thoughts.

You have recovered very well from the miscarriage. Unfortunately the prognosis for any future pregnancy is not promising. Because of the damage to your hip, the subsequent tilting of your uterus, there is only a one-in-ten chance you could successfully conceive....

Conflicting messages fought for attention in her mind. She waited for the sorrow, the envy. Surprisingly, it didn't materialize.

Linda was having another baby. It was wonderful, and a little painful, but the closest thing to having one of her own. "You know I'm happy for you, sis. But—"

"The boys have begged me to let them tell you. Please say you'll come." With a smile in her voice, Linda sweetened the pot. "You could bring John along."

"I don't know," Jenny hedged. She did feel isolated, but she wasn't sure she wanted to ask John to take her to Linda and Wayne's. In addition to the impromptu tour he'd given her of Fort Riley a week before, he'd also delivered her to the hospital for therapy and stopped by to check on her a few times. For two weeks he'd been trying to do things for her, acting like any good friend, or even a brother. So why was it driving her up the wall?

Because of the phone calls. He called her every night—usually right before she went to bed. And every night she went to sleep with the sound of his voice in her ears, her imagination running rampant. What would it be like to go to sleep in his arms, to wake up to his kiss?

She had the intense urge to push him beyond his control. To ignore promises and any other future but today. Right now.

A dizzying blitz of panic rushed through her. Linda was only suggesting dinner; it was her own imagination she had to worry about. Fantasies like the ones she had woven into the letters whirled through her mind, affecting her body, her sanity. But now new elements had been added—a voice, a face, a pair of steady gray eyes.

"Hello? Anybody home?" Linda was laughing. "Yes or no?"

Jenny had to force her thoughts back to the original conversation. "I'll mention it to him when he calls."

"I WANT TO WATCH YOU eat with chopsticks." John purposely spoke low into the phone, making his suggestion sound like a perversion.

Jenny laughed. "Sounds messy."

"Hey, if you can handle crutches, you can handle chopsticks. And I'd be there to back you up."

A long moment of silence followed, and John wondered if he'd inadvertently stomped on her good mood. He wished he was looking into her eyes. "Are you still there?"

"Uh-huh."

"So what do you say? Tomorrow night. Seven-thirty." He wanted her to get used to being with him. To go out on a real, Saturday-night date. To somehow get past this unfulfilling friendship thing.

"I don't think so."

John had to stop and take a deep breath. Her answer surprised him, and he didn't like surprises. "Why not?"

"Maybe another night."

"Why, Jenny?" He had to know. She'd been fine until he asked her to go to dinner. Now she seemed distant, different, and he needed to know why.

Jenny's thoughts were scrambled. Why? She couldn't tell him it was because she was afraid. Part of her wanted to let him into her life and see if there weren't some things they could share. Without warning the memory of his well-worn running shoes jolted her thoughts and slammed the door shut on that idea.

"I think I've been overdoing a little lately." Jenny looked down toward the one crutch resting at her feet and winced at the lie. "I don't want another setback." She ran a hand through her hair and shut her eyes. Why was she such a coward?

"I could get the food to go." His words were light, but the humor had faded. "The chopsticks come in those little paper wrappers—"

"I'd like that, but some other night." Jenny cut him off before the solid lump of sorrow and guilt wedged in her throat could make her cry.

"SO WHAT'S THE DEAL with you and John?" With his usual lack of tact, Wayne got right to the point.

Jenny looked out of the car window at the rolling, green land they were passing, wishing for once that she lived closer to her sister. A thirty-minute interrogation from Wayne would not improve her mood.

"What do you mean?"

"I mean, he's always been a straight-ahead guy—first man in, last man out. But lately—" Wayne shot her a meaningful sideways glance "—he's leaving work a little early or disappearing at lunchtime. This is definitely not normal behavior for Braithwaite."

"Why do you think it has anything to do with me?"

"Tell me it doesn't."

Jenny sighed, surrendering. "All right, he's given me a ride to therapy and stopped by the house a few times. Is that what you want to know?"

"No. I want to know what you intend to do about him. I know that Linda asked you to invite him tonight, and I also know he was still at work when I left." Wayne glanced in her direction again. "I started this whole thing, and I don't like the idea of my buddy getting hurt by it."

Jenny was startled by his words. The timbre of Wayne's voice was absolutely serious.

"I don't want to hurt him. I . . ." She'd wanted to put some distance between them, and spending the evening at Linda and Wayne's with him seemed so significant. "I think he's a great guy, but—"

"But you're not interested," Wayne finished for her.

A few notes of choked laughter escaped before Jenny got herself under control. Not interested! She was so interested she didn't know how to act around John anymore. If she gave in to all the tumbling feelings he set in motion, and then John decided he couldn't handle her physical limitations, he could just walk away. *She* couldn't. She had to live with her limitations. She couldn't give the future a test drive to see if she liked it. "I wouldn't exactly say *not* interested," she managed to respond.

Wayne maneuvered the car onto the shoulder of the road and coasted to a stop before he braced one arm on the steering wheel and turned to her. "Look, I know you've been hurt, and you have every right to be confused. But I just want to tell you one thing. John is nothing like Randy. John's the kind of man any officer would want on his flank. He takes care of his own." Wayne straightened and prepared to steer the car back onto the road. "The rest is between the two of you."

WHAT WAS JOHN DOING? Was he home, or had he gone out for Chinese food with someone else? A shimmer of panic ran through her. She didn't really expect him to hang around forever, did she? To spend his Saturday nights alone?

Jenny flinched when Linda walked through the kitchen door carrying a cake with a sparkler in it. The two boys trailed behind their mother nearly dancing with excitement.

Finally Tommy could contain himself no longer, bursting out, "We're gonna have a baby!"

"A baby?" Jenny went along with the surprise. "Really?"

Linda moved to Wayne's side and put an arm around her husband. "Just barely. The baby, that is. I'm never late without good reason. So I did one of those early test things." She kissed Wayne's jaw near his ear. "This baby is our welcome-home gift. Last one, I promise."

Wayne's fingers trapped Linda's hand—probably so she couldn't punch him—as he frowned like a man with important wisdom to impart. "You know, I think I've finally figured out what's causing it."

"*Wayne.*" Linda's voice, full of warning, only widened his grin.

Jenny looked into her sister's sparkling eyes and felt a wave of happiness. Home. Husband. A baby. She picked up her water glass for a toast. "Well, congratulations." She didn't have to force her smile as she quipped, "And, of course, welcome home."

SHE WASN'T HOME. John stared at the front of Jenny's house feeling like one of the world's biggest fools. His truck keys bit into the palm of his hand like jagged pieces of glass. Hadn't she told him she was staying home? *No*, his mind taunted, *she told you she didn't want to go out with you.*

He'd been so worried when he called and she hadn't answered. He'd immediately thought something was wrong, that she needed help. After rushing over to her house in a panic he'd discovered she was out. Without him. A shocking sense of desolation moved through him. Fury followed. With stiff, angry movements he got back into his truck and started the engine. *The hell with it! She can—*

Headlights flashed in the rearview mirror. A car pulled in the driveway behind his and John realized that a man was driving, and that Jenny was sitting next to him.

Icy calm settled over John. His fingers moved to the keys, and the engine of his truck went silent. *Don't get out of the truck, John,* the commander in his brain ordered. *If you get out of the truck you'll do something crazy. She doesn't belong to you. She never said . . .*

Car doors opened. Light bloomed in the interior of the car. John's gut twisted at the image of her with another man, but his attention was glued on Jenny. She didn't move; she simply sat and stared. She looked shocked...and guilty. And all he wanted to do was yank her out of that car and kiss her until she couldn't talk.

A hand slapped the back of his truck. "You waiting for a bus, or what?" Wayne's voice drifted to him through the pounding of his anger.

John rubbed his forehead as if he could ease the mayhem in his mind. His logic had been so completely staggered by the unexpected stab of jealousy that he hadn't recognized Wayne. He drew in a deep breath, then opened the door.

His whole body felt rigid, the result of anger and pain. He suddenly knew he'd stepped off the edge of a precipice without ever seeing it. This woman could hurt him, without effort or intent, deeper and harder than anyone had ever hurt him before. All she had to do was say no.

Jenny met him between the car bumpers. He couldn't subdue a rush of admiration. She was down to one crutch again and moving pretty well. He had to suck in a breath and plunge his hands into his pockets to keep up the pretence that he was unaffected by the look on her face.

She was glad to see him. In the dim light her eyes looked deep blue, but there was an unmistakable shine of happiness, of eagerness. Before he knew it, one of his hands escaped to brush against her cheek and ruffle her bright hair.

He cleared his throat. "Hey."

"Hey, yourself."

Why didn't she ask what he was doing there, parked in her driveway at eleven-thirty in the evening? "I called and you didn't answer and I—"

"I'm sorry." Her gaze skittered toward Wayne. "I didn't expect to be so late."

"It's all our fault," Wayne confessed. "We got carried away celebrating."

"Celebrating?"

Jenny shifted her crutch to a more comfortable position. "Linda and Wayne are going to have another baby."

John extended his hand to Wayne. "Another Dixon to plague the universe?"

Wayne grinned at the insult and shook John's hand. "Yeah, well, we've got room for one more, and Linda wants a girl."

"Congratulations."

"Thanks, man." Wayne gave John a shrewd look. "Listen, can you get Jenny settled inside? I need to get on the road."

John tried not to act too eager as he took Jenny's bag from Wayne. "Sure. No problem." He was still standing there just looking at her when Wayne's lights faded into the night.

"Did you go out for Chinese?" Jenny's voice sounded hesitant. She made no move toward the house.

Chinese? He tried to remember what he'd done besides pace and wonder and, finally, act. He hadn't eaten at all. "No, I, uh, picked up a hamburger," he lied.

She stepped forward. "I wondered what you decided to do. I figured you wouldn't be up for dinner at Linda and Wayne's."

The words almost sounded like an apology. Why hadn't she asked him?

"Why would you figure that?" He fell into step beside her.

She stopped and turned to face him. "I just thought—" She seemed to search for words. The ones she found hit him like a shot of one-hundred-proof whiskey. "I wish you'd been there. I missed you."

John swallowed. The memory of the entire miserable, heart-wrenching evening he'd just spent burned right out of his mind. It was worth it, all the pain and uncertainty, to be standing in the darkness hearing her say she'd missed him.

"All you have to do is ask, remember?"

She nodded slowly. "I remember." Her eyes seemed to be asking a question, a very important question. "I'm working up to it."

"Good," he said, nearly choking.

He took her arm and started her toward the house again. He was determined not to spoil everything by trying to kiss her. He wasn't sure he'd be able to stop. His voice emerged low and strained. "Just don't expect me to be magnanimous and say 'take your time.'"

When they reached the door, Jenny searched through her bag for the keys, then unlocked the dead bolt. John turned the handle and swung the door open. A light illuminated the hallway, but the rest of the house was dark. He waited for Jenny to cross the threshold.

"Do you want me to check under the bed for you?" He smiled but Jenny thought he looked nervous, hesitant to make himself at home.

"That won't be necessary."

"Well . . ." He glanced over his shoulder, as if to see whether or not his truck was still there. "I guess I—" He slipped his hands into his pockets again. "Listen, how about if I stop by tomorrow? I could take you to lunch or something."

Or something . . . Jenny smiled. That's what friends did. They went to lunch or something. "Sure," she answered.

But he didn't leave. Jenny's fingers shifted with the sudden urge to touch him, to simply acknowledge his presence in her life. Her left hand came to rest on his chest, over the solid beat of his heart.

"John?"

He seemed poised on the edge of some decision. "Yeah?"

Now what? Jenny wondered. She had his complete and undivided attention. She could feel it through his shirt. All she had to do was say, "Kiss me, John," and he would. Or "Please stay, John...."

"Would you kiss me, please?"

A slow smile spread across his face. "I'd be happy to, ma'am."

One of his large, warm hands slipped around the nape of her neck as she lifted her mouth. She drew in one quick breath before his lips met hers.

His lips were moist and warm, and it seemed perfectly natural to meet the first tentative touch of his tongue with her own. He stepped closer and her hand slid around his neck, pulling him downward, inward. He coaxed her lips open wider and delved deeper. The searching caress of his tongue sent a shudder of longing shooting from Jenny's mouth to her knees. The hand at the small of her back that had been urging her nearer abruptly ceased to push. His fingers made a lazy circle against the fabric of her blouse as he gradually drew back from the kiss. He freed her mouth but remained close enough to draw the same breath of air Jenny was trying to find.

"Anything else I can do for you?" The silken suggestion of his words tingled through her mind while his breath caressed her jaw. He kissed her chin quickly before his mouth hovered over hers, waiting.

Jenny wanted to be kissed again. She pulled him closer until their mouths met. His lips were warmer, she decided. Her own felt wetter, more pliant. Why had she ever been afraid of this? The kiss began gently, then quickly changed into a hungry, searching quest.

The telephone rang shrilly, fracturing the charged silence between them. Startled, Jenny pulled back. John's arms remained tight around her; his heart seemed to be pounding in her ears. She felt vulnerable, exposed, unable to decide if she was grateful for the interruption or furious. "That's probably Linda checking to see that I'm all right." Her voice sounded ragged and small.

John nodded and slowly loosened his arms, backing away to a safer distance. Jenny fought a potent attack of disappointment.

The phone rang again.

She caught his hand as it slid away from her. "I guess I'll see you tomorrow, then."

His fingers closed around hers, tightly, for a second. He exhaled like a man who has found his footing on shaky ground. "That's a bet you won't lose." A kaleidoscope of emotion swirled in the gray eyes that held her gaze—heat and uncertainty, serious intent and lecherous promise. Jenny's pulse beat in an odd rhythm as his silent spell vibrated through her, touching places that had no defense.

The phone rang a third time.

With a mock salute and a smile that looked regretful he said, "Good night."

She could barely force an answer through her throat as he closed the door.

Jenny reached the telephone by the fifth ring. She answered without much enthusiasm. "Hello?" The lights from John's truck illuminated the curtains as he backed out of the driveway. Jenny pushed the curtain aside and watched his taillights recede.

"Hi, Jen." The voice on the phone didn't belong to Linda. Feeling as though someone had yanked the carpet from beneath her feet, Jenny let go of the curtain and leaned heavily against the back of the couch. Why were some days designed like tests?

"Hello, Randy."

"I've been trying to get you all night."

The phone line sang with the echo of long distance. Jenny could hear people talking in the background. She had an uncomfortable attack of déjà vu. How many times during their marriage had Randy called her from some hotel room halfway across the country? Called to tell her the soccer team had won, or lost. Called to make her feel better about his being away, or to assuage a guilty conscience. In the beginning she'd believed he was phoning from his own room. By his second season with the team she was never sure.

Jenny realized she didn't miss those obligatory calls.

"Sorry," she said, purposely keeping her tone light and unconcerned. "I was out."

"Out?" He sounded incredulous. After a few seconds of silence he said, "Well, great! I heard you were getting around better."

"I'm doing fine. Is that why you called? To see how I'm doing?" Jenny frowned at her sarcasm. She hadn't meant it to be so obvious. Neither of them had put forth much effort to save their marriage. She'd been consumed, physically and mentally, by the accident. It had taken all her concentration and determination to overcome the worst-case diagnosis the doctors had originally given her. And Randy had been out the door when he learned that he might have to look after an invalid wife.

"I called because we need to talk about some things."
Wariness invaded his voice. "I'll be back in Kansas City
on Monday. Can I see you?" Male laughter erupted in the
background and a female voice said, "Bye."

"What is this about?" Jenny asked, afraid that some
leftover sense of guilt was nagging him to make amends.
She didn't want to have to deal with Randy now. He belonged to the past, and she didn't want to give him the
opportunity to disrupt the progress she had worked so
hard for. *Poor Jenny*. She didn't want to see that expression on his face again.

John never looked at her that way. Jenny's spine
straightened with new resolve. She could tell Randy she
didn't need his help or pity. She was just fine.

"I don't want to get into it over the phone," he said in
a low voice, as if he were worried about being over-
heard. "I need to talk to you face-to-face." More male
laughter and a loud blast of music. "Can I stop by on
Monday?" Randy seemed unusually serious in the midst
of what was obviously a party.

Jenny sighed and left him waiting for an answer while
she decided what to do.

"Hey, you guys, turn that down for a minute. I'm on
the phone! Jen? What?"

"I didn't say anything," she answered, gripping the
receiver harder. It was so typical for him to call and ask
a question, then not be able to hear the answer.

"All right," she agreed, finally. "But make it Tuesday,
after three."

"Good. I'll see you then." He didn't sound as if it was
good at all. "I'm glad you're better," he said. "Really!"
The last word was practically shouted over the sound of
the music.

"Thanks!" Jenny raised her voice to match his. "Bye!"

Jenny hung up the phone, shaking her head. Funny how her entire world could change while Randy's stayed exactly the same. Actually, it wasn't very funny at all. It was pretty sad—for Randy.

For the first time since the accident Jenny knew her life, in some ways, might be better than it had been before. Before she was injured, before she realized how fragile normalcy could be. Now she'd never take anything for granted. Not her friends, or her family, or even the years she had left to live. And she would never spend her time waiting or worrying about what someone else might decide concerning her future. She would make the decisions and find her own peace. She would simply get on with it. She wanted . . .

John. He seemed to be all around her, in the letters, in her dreams, in her arms. . . . It would be foolish to take him for granted, no matter what his intentions turned out to be.

Maybe she *was* ready to ask.

12

John,
I had the oil changed in the car as you suggested, but then I parked it under the oak tree in front of the house. Remember how the birds love to perch in that tree? Now the car needs to be washed and waxed.

I'll get to it, I promise. The next sunny day we have, when I'm restless, unable to sit still. When the dull pain of missing you gathers into a physical ache that demands relief. I'll go out and scrub that car until I'm too tired to think or to want. Too tired to do anything but sleep and search for you in my dreams.

Jenny

"HAVE YOU GOT A HOSE connection in the front yard?" John asked, initiating the first step of his seduction campaign.

"Yeah, why?"

"A bucket and an old rag?"

Jenny looked as if she had missed the announcement of a game of twenty questions. "In the utility room, through the kitchen."

John couldn't help smiling. She looked so left out. "May I borrow them?" Before she could answer, he sat down and went to work on the laces of his sneakers.

"Sure," she answered. "What are you going to do?"

"It's a beautiful day outside." One of his shoes thudded to the rug. The sock followed. "I thought I'd wash your car. Want to help?" The other shoe and sock joined the pile.

"Wash my car?" Jenny's eyes were riveted on his bare feet. He glanced down to make sure they hadn't mutated into fins. He wiggled his toes. They looked perfectly normal to him. What was she so interested in? He stood and began unbuttoning his shirt. If she thought his toes were riveting, then he'd give her something else to stare at.

"That is your car in the driveway, isn't it? The dusty blue Toyota?"

"Yes . . . I, uh . . ." Jenny was having some difficulty following the conversation. She'd never before realized how intimate the simple action of removing shoes could be. But these were John's shoes, she reminded herself, John's laces pulled loose by his strong fingers, John's bare feet planted on her carpet as if they belonged there. Then her gaze traveled up his long legs to his hands. He was taking off his shirt. A wave of longing ran under her skin. He stood there, stripping out of his clothes, as if she was invisible. Or worse, as if she was his audience.

All through lunch he had been different, quiet, thoughtful. More brotherly than usual. Now he'd changed. His hands moved more slowly, his eyes held challenge. His mouth . . .

"Maybe you should change," he said as he tossed his shirt over the back of the nearest chair. His T-shirt followed.

She was in catatonic shock. Her eyes were locked on his bare chest, on the smooth skin darkened by the desert sun. On the soft scattering of dark hair that tapered downward.

Her cheeks felt hot enough to toast bread. How could he sound so nonchalant when she was on fire? How could she sit and watch him undress without touching? Without knowing if his skin smelled like sunshine or midnight. If it would be as familiar as her dreams.

She realized she'd missed whatever he'd just said. "What?" She had to push the word through her throat and force her eyes to meet his.

"You might get your sweats wet," he said.

John couldn't stop the knowing smile from appearing. The warmth in her gaze felt like the sun against his skin. Before he was finished she would be putty in his hands. If he could keep his hands off her that long. She looked so vulnerable with her brows crinkled by a perplexed look.

He'd waited through lunch, the perfect friend, making conversation he couldn't remember, smiling when she smiled, eating food he hadn't really tasted. Now they were alone, and he wanted nothing more than to walk over and pull her into his arms, to know if her skin was like velvet, her mouth like . . . He had to stop the images cascading through his mind. Who was seducing whom? He determinedly strode past her toward the kitchen. "I'll get the bucket."

The day was beautiful, warmer than usual for early May, with freshly cut grass scenting the air. John carried a lawn chair and set it near the driveway. By the time Jenny was settled in the chair she'd regained her equilibrium. John filled the bucket, wet down the car and returned to her with the hose.

"You take up a defensive position," he said with mock solemnity, "and be officer in charge of the hose."

"I don't know," she said as her hands closed around the gunlike nozzle. "Are you sure you trust me with such an important job?"

His smile could have melted stainless steel. "I trust you."

Well, you shouldn't, she thought, mesmerized by that smile. He seemed to read her mind. With a wink he walked away.

What was he doing, winking at her? Only Drew winked at her. John had obviously picked up some bad habits at the hospital. Bad habits. Jenny felt like groaning. Staring at John had become a habit. The simple act of watching him wash her car was turning into torture, and all because she couldn't take her eyes off him. The way the muscles of his back moved and stretched as he scrubbed the roof of the car. The way his pants molded his thighs and rear when he squatted to reach the side panels.

She'd demanded they stay *friends.* Did friends drive other friends crazy with a smile and a wink? With the innocent act of washing a car? She had certainly never felt anything like this toward Drew, and he winked at her all the time. Not even Randy had set her nerves on fire like John did. Randy had been her husband, her lover. The implication was sobering. So John had kissed her a few times. A few kisses shouldn't transform her into a blithering fool. Her wayward mind drifted to the memory of his mouth, the firm, smooth possession of his lips....

The afternoon had a heavy, hazy quality. An insect flew by her face, and she absently waved it away. She felt as if she were lost in a dream.

Half the car was covered by soapsuds before he returned for the hose. Backlit by the sun, the stream of water he sprayed from the nozzle scattered like a thousand diamonds. Time seemed to slow and shift. But after a few moments she held the hose securely again.

The insect reappeared, making a landing on her bare arm. The hazy afternoon suddenly snapped into sharp focus. Yellow and black. A bee. With an involuntary yelp Jenny surged to her feet to dislodge the menace, using the chair for support. It was simply reflexes that made her squirt the buzzing offender with the hose.

John's head snapped up at Jenny's exclamation of alarm. He turned toward her just in time to receive the full force of the water in the center of his chest. The impact of the cold water was such a shock he sucked in a deep breath but didn't move. After one drenching moment, Jenny dropped the sprayer.

And started laughing.

John wanted to laugh, too, but he was too wet and too stunned. "What the hell—"

"I didn't mean— There was a bee—" Jenny gasped, nearly bent double with laughter. But when John came toward her, she decided to retreat. For a heartbeat she seemed to forget her injury and turned to run. John reached her in three lunging strides, catching her as she lost her balance.

"Oh, no, you don't!" he demanded. He couldn't look at her, remind her that she'd almost fallen, so he did the first thing any other person would do after being drenched. He enveloped her in a soggy hug and rubbed his face against her cheek and hair like a wet dog after a bath. He didn't allow her any breathing room until he was sure his expression wouldn't show his worry. If she'd fallen...

Steady on her feet, thanks to John, Jenny wasn't laughing anymore. She was out of breath, out of excuses and out of room to retreat. John's persistent presence in her life surrounded her senses as completely as the taut muscles of his arms surrounded her body. His skin smelled like soap and sunshine, spiced by his faint aftershave. The feel of his breath along her ear and neck sent hair-raising tremors through her. His heart seemed to be pounding inside her own chest.

After the initial surprise of his soaking embrace, she realized she was pressing toward him rather than pulling away. It took him less than a moment to realize it, too. He went still.

Jenny slowly raised her gaze to his. He looked fierce instead of playful, as if he would rather be shaking her until her teeth rattled than wrestling in good humor. A queer shiver of anticipation overtook her.

"I know what you want from me, and I—"

"You have no idea what I want from you," he interrupted, frowning as if he wasn't sure himself. "But I'll take whatever you're offering."

"I have scars." The words tumbled out. "And I don't know if I can—"

"I don't care." His eyes held hers, waiting, willing her to say the words.

Her gaze dropped to his lips.

"I want..." She raised her mouth as her eyelids drifted downward. "Please."

John stared at the blatant longing on Jenny's face and felt a savage, soaring exhilaration, as if he'd jumped off a building and suddenly grown wings. *You win, old buddy.* God, he'd waited so long. Her lips were moist and soft and willing. They opened under the pressure of his, slowly, irresistibly. An invitation he couldn't pass up. His tongue traced the shape of her lower lip, then dipped inside to taste and linger.

A breeze raised goose bumps on John's wet skin, but he was lost in Jenny's mouth, Jenny's heat. He didn't think he would ever be cold again.

He shifted her in his arms, preparing to pick her up, but she resisted, dragging her mouth free of his. "What are you doing?"

His arm slipped under her thighs. "I'm carrying you into the house. To a bed."

"No," she said quickly, urgently. Her hands tightened on his shoulders, urging him to release her.

John straightened and looked down at her. Was she afraid again? Would she deny what was happening, what was *going* to happen between them?

She held his gaze steadily, without fear. She tried to smile. "I can walk." Her arm slipped around his waist. "Walk with me."

JOHN CLOSED THE FRONT door behind them. The finality of his action seemed to stiffen Jenny's spine. She hesitated. He ran a hand slowly down her back and pulled her around to face him. He wanted to tease her, to chase away the look of impending doom that had fallen over her. But the wistful uncertainty of her expression engulfed him like a wave of liquid heat. Never mind teasing. He had to kiss her again.

His mouth found hers with heartfelt intention. He wanted her melting and mindless. So hot that she would never forget the lingering invasion of his kiss, the determined gentleness of his touch. So mindless that she wouldn't remember her fears or her scars—or any other man.

She tasted like sweet lemonade on a scorching day. But instead of quenching his thirst she only made him want to drink deeper to savor every drop. A bright haze seemed to fill his mind. He had to have more of her.

Jenny couldn't breathe, and she didn't want to. She felt a tremor in John's arms as they tightened around her and she gave herself to the kiss, to the man. His tongue touched hers, then retreated, making both her legs go weak with anticipation, making her silently swear to surrender anything so long as he didn't stop. His lips coaxed hers open wider for better access before his tongue returned. When she ventured into her own exploration of his mouth, he caught the tip of her tongue in a sucking motion. The eroticism of that one tiny action sent an ache of raw, toe-curling need through her. Need that blossomed into a whimper Jenny heard but couldn't identify as her own. With an answering curse, John relinquished her mouth.

He pressed his cheek against hers. "Where's your room? Your bed?" he demanded, his voice low and harsh. She had never heard him sound that way. He was so familiar to her, yet she'd never known him like this. This man was a stranger, a seductive mystery who seemed to be burning up. His skin felt like fire. Before she could answer, his hands swept down her back and he hauled her to him, aligning her hips with his. Heat leaped across the meager barrier of their clothes. Jenny stretched upward, pressing closer, higher, hotter. She sucked in a breath as his hands slipped underneath the band of her sweatshirt and splayed across her bare back. In mindless anticipation she moved her mouth toward his.

"Where?" he said again, tantalizing her by avoiding the kiss.

"Second door on the right."

Without stopping for argument John swept her up in his arms and carried her through the door.

He set her gently on her feet beside her bed. Never re-linquishing his possessive hold, he pulled her sweatshirt upward. When she hesitated, he kissed her hair and her ear. "Please," he whispered, "I want to feel you against me."

Jenny couldn't find *no* in her vocabulary. Not when his hands were moving over her, not when he sounded as though he would die if she refused.

She raised her arms, and before the sweatshirt settled on the floor he was kissing her again.

Lost in the now-familiar seduction of his mouth, Jenny felt a tug a second before her bra fell away. Then, slowly, he moved closer, placing her arms around his neck, pressing bare chest to bare breasts.

Jenny gave herself up to the exquisite sensation of warm and smooth against hot and rough. She moved, gliding along the wall of his chest, savoring the friction. John's fingers dug into her back. "Jenny," he murmured before claiming another kiss, a rougher, more urgent kiss.

Then he was arching her backward, kissing her neck, her shoulder while he cupped one of her breasts, ready-ing it for his mouth. When his lips closed over the ach-ing center and his tongue found her hardened nipple, Jenny gasped. His mouth was so warm. It had been so long. Her breath caught. *And it was never like this.*

John sank onto the side of the bed and positioned her between his spread thighs. His fingers worked the draw-string of her sweatpants while his mouth tasted and nuz-zled her skin.

A surge of alarm ran through Jenny as she felt the pull at her waist. It was one thing to be normal and naked and making love in the afternoon sun. But she wasn't nor-mal, and being naked was quite another thing when it meant exposing her scars in the unforgiving light of day. Her hands moved to stop him.

At her show of resistance, John slid his arms around her waist, pressed his face to her stomach and went still. The tickle of his breath and the rapid rise and fall of his shoulders sent a sinuous flutter of longing through Jenny. She fanned her fingers into the dark, minklike silk of his closely cropped hair. Her body relished every touch, every sensation, but her mind scrambled for control, for reassurance. *Please understand*, she pleaded silently.

After a moment he raised his eyes to meet her gaze. He didn't look angry. On the contrary, there was an unmistakable twinkle in his eyes.

His hands rested on her hips, and one finger insinuated itself inside the waistband of her sweats to casually stroke the skin beneath. "Hon," he said with an air of innocent gravity, "we can't do this unless we take these off."

She tried to be mad at him or at least defensive, but he looked so charming and expectant she couldn't stop her mouth from quirking into a smile.

"Are you making fun of me?" she accused in mock severity. She stared into John's turbulent gray eyes as all the amusement faded from his features.

His hands tightened on her waist. "No, Jenny. I'm not making fun of you." He took a deep breath, then let it out slowly. His expression was bleak. "I'm about to fly into five hundred pieces because I want you so bad." His thighs flexed, pressing her knees closer, trapping, then releasing. "You're going to have to trust me. I won't look at you if you don't want me to, but it doesn't matter what you look like under these." He plucked at the waistband of her sweats. "Nothing will ever stop me from wanting you."

She believed him. Yet the fear wouldn't let go. Randy's defection had hurt her, but a rejection from John would be more than she could stand.

She cradled his face against her stomach to escape those serious gray eyes. The slight rasp of his stubble produced a jaw-tightening, sensual quake that raced through her.

"I want to do this," Jenny whispered, closing her eyes as the back draft of pure need flowed over her. Lord! How she wanted to do this, right now, and with this remarkable man. She wanted to be normal for him, to be beautiful for him....

But she wasn't. "I just can't—"

"Shh," John interrupted, pulling away. Jenny experienced one moment of heart-stopping fear. Was he going to leave?

"No, please..." Her voice came out in a strained croak.

John didn't seem to hear. He was on his feet, yanking back the bed cover. Holding up one corner of the sheet, he nudged her toward the bed. "You can take them off under there." He smiled, but the twinkle was missing from his eyes. "Then...it's every man for himself."

He dropped the sheet and bent over her. "You get naked," he ordered, and kissed her hurriedly on the mouth.

The sheets were cool against her bare breasts, the bed empty except for her nearly normal body and her illusive dreams. The thought of John leaving her, of being alone, threatened to engulf her. She pushed the unpleasant qualm away, fighting for the pleasure of today without fear of the future—or the past. One specific, luminous dream rose like swirling smoke in her memory. A dream about John touching her, loving her. Dreams didn't come true, did they? Her hands untangled the drawstring of her sweats and she pushed the last barrier down her legs. She wanted to find out, right *now*.

John pulled his wallet from his back pocket, extracted a colorful package and tossed both on the table next to the bed. His weight depressed the mattress as he stretched out beside her. Without a word he slipped an arm under her shoulders and buried his face in her hair. His agitated breathing telegraphed shivers of renewed heat under her skin. He held her as if he'd been searching for her everywhere and had finally found her. He kissed her ear, while his hand began a leisurely journey over the sheet, skimming her breast, then downward to her hip.

"Are you . . ." He didn't finish the question. His lips covered hers, jumbling her senses with a hot, open-mouthed kiss. The sheet fell to her waist as he pulled her upward. Her fingers grazed his ribs, then shaped the muscles of his back as she pressed closer.

This was no dream, this was real—he was real. And at that moment she wanted him beyond all caution, beyond all care.

"I like the way you smell. . . ." He nuzzled her neck, then nipped the soft skin of her shoulder with his teeth. "The way you taste." He looked into her eyes as if he wanted to promise her anything. "I'll try to go slow but I . . ."

"John." She slid her palm along his cheek. The slight roughness triggered a sweet tightening along the inside of her arm and a tingling across her breasts. "I've been afraid of other things," she said, staring into the depths of his gray eyes. "But I've never been afraid of you."

He caught her wrist and turned to kiss her palm. "You've got to tell me if I hurt you. Will you do that?"

She nodded.

He kissed her palm once more before releasing her, then turned away in order to strip off his pants. A moment later he was sliding under the cool sheet, gathering her to him.

The contact was devastating, hotter and rougher than any dream. More real. More demanding. No time for gentle laughter and hesitant touches. John's mouth settled on hers with straightforward concentration, and Jenny answered with a ferocity that astonished them both.

He kissed her until she was light-headed, her mind unable to focus. Too much oxygen. No, not enough. Too much sensation. His breath fanned her face as his fingers squeezed the soft skin of her back, then skimmed over her ribs with a feather touch. No, not enough. Jenny drew in more air and arched toward his hand as he gently circled, then shaped her breast.

She broke away from his mouth when his thumb brushed her nipple and it tightened to a straining peak.

"John—" She closed her eyes and twisted toward him, toward his hands, his mouth. He made a consoling sound, a sort of mumbled answer, but his lips were touching her shoulder, the sensitive skin of her neck, the side of her breast. His tongue replaced his thumb, elevating the sweet torture to a new and excruciating level. Jenny's restless fingers tightened their grip on his muscular shoulders. She wanted to press him closer, but John seemed to have lost all urgency. He teased and tickled and sucked, first one nipple, then the other as if he had a lifetime to spend in exploration.

She had no control over the havoc he was stirring. It felt too good. Too good to do anything but strain toward him and follow where he was taking the two of them. She had to touch him, to make him feel what she was feeling. Her fingers trailed over the overheated skin of his chest. The teasing brush of hair tantalized her fingertips, then the hard nub of his nipple.

Demand shot through John once again. He broke away from his playful torment and captured her mouth in a kiss that forced her head backward and caused her to grasp his hips in order to keep him close.

A new kind of pleasure captured her senses. She slipped one hand along the taut flatness of his belly, following the soft line of hair downward. Caressing him, feeling his skin quiver under her fingers, produced a corresponding pulse deep within her.

Suddenly his body moved, pinning her hand between his belly and her hip. She could feel the heat and thickness of his erection against her leg. He dragged his mouth from hers. "Don't—" He didn't give her time for rebuttal. He drew in a deep, agitated breath and closed his eyes. "You're not ready yet." She could feel his heart pounding against her. "And I'm about three klicks past reason."

He pulled back to look down into Jenny's blue eyes framed by her tousled blond hair. The sight caused his heart to stutter and skip, and nearly stole his breath. She looked playful, thoroughly disheveled, and, at the risk of waxing poetic, he decided she looked bold.

She wants this, wants me.

It was the last coherent thought he recognized. Balanced on one elbow, he ran his left hand along her arm, to her belly, then insinuated it between their bodies until he found the wetness between her thighs. She moaned in reaction and pressed closer, opening, offering. He kissed her and stroked her until she moaned again, until he was dangerously close to exploding on his own.

"John—"

No more waiting. The urgency of Jenny's voice echoed through him. He paused and put on the one thing that had to stand between them. Then he nudged her thighs apart with his knees. The first sweet, gliding stroke of entry took him down like a leg sweep. A stunning spasm of pleasure thrummed through his body. She was so hot, so tight. He felt himself pulse inside her.

As if in answer to his need, his strained stillness, Jenny moved upward to meet his thrust. Her nails grazed the sensitive skin near his spine, forcing him closer. Her warm breath whispered along his neck.

He drew in a gulp of air, held it, then let it out in a rush. "Hon—be still, just for a—" But it was too late. He had to move, to push. With a groan of defeat, his mouth smothered hers as he drove into her fast and hard.

Dimly he felt Jenny fight her way free of the kiss. Then she gasped and arched beneath him, crying out a fraction of a second before the shuddering rush of climax overtook him. John's mind went blank as his body, suspended on the brink, coiled with the immobilizing current of gratification rolling through him.

Then, after an eternity, rational thought returned.

"Son of a bitch!" The angry words snarled into the pillow took Jenny by surprise. The sensual glow surrounding her faltered.

A shudder went through the muscle of John's arm before he pushed off her. "Damn it to—"

In one smooth motion he rolled onto his back, pulling her close to his side. He shoved his face against her neck. "Did I hurt you?" His hands gripped her tightly for a moment, then loosened, as if he feared he'd break her. He cleared his throat, either to catch his breath or to find his normal voice. *"Did I?"*

Jenny gently urged his head upward with her hands so she could see his eyes. "I'm fine." She slid her arm across his chest until her breasts were pressed to his ribs. "I'm terrific." She smiled languidly.

He drew her closer and sighed. "God. I thought I hurt you. I forgot..." He looked puzzled, shocked. He closed his eyes and shook his head. "I just lost it."

His words produced a different sort of shock in Jenny. Unwittingly he'd given her a gift beyond description—the ultimate proof. When she was in his arms, when he was deep inside her, he forgot she wasn't perfect.

Jenny lightly kissed his lips, then lowered her head to his shoulder. She wasn't ready to face the frightening rush of tenderness filling her heart. *Keep it light*, her logic ordered.

"Do you suppose we could stay like this for about a year or so?" she murmured.

John kissed her cheek and ran one hand through her ruffled hair. "All you have to do is ask," he replied as he pulled the sheet up over them.

JENNY SLOWLY OPENED her eyes an hour later, wondering why she felt so good. It must have been the dream, the... It took only a few seconds to realize she wasn't dreaming. The warm, definitely male body that was sliding under the sheets, aligning itself along her backside, was real. Pleasure washed over her again. She stretched lazily, then snuggled closer to John. A heavy arm draped over her waist, then shifted. A slow hand ran down her hip. She caught her breath when the fingers traced the line of one of her scars.

John's low voice vibrated close to her ear. "Are you awake?" The hand on her thigh slid inward and upward, scattering any trepidation about his reaction to her scars. She could feel the evidence of his interest pressed along her back, thick and hot. Whatever he thought about her injury certainly had no effect on his libido.

"Uh-huh," was all she could manage. Jenny stretched again and brazenly rubbed herself against him. Strong teeth nipped the side of her neck. Payback. She could get to like this.

His hand slid over her injured hip and thigh once more. "Are you sure we didn't hurt your leg?"

Jenny bent her knee, then straightened it. "Yes, I'm sure. It feels fine." A slow smile curved her lips. "I feel great." She extended one arm upward, looped it around his neck and pulled his face forward for an awkward kiss. She ended up on her back with him bending over her.

"I think I better check it, just to be sure." He kissed her nose, her chin. He shouldered the sheet down and kissed the center of her chest, over her heart. The soft rush of his breath caused her nipples to strain and harden in anticipation. She watched him smile before he kissed one, then the other.

The sheet somehow got twisted around his leg and by the time he was free, it had fallen below her waist.

He kissed her stomach, circled her belly button with his tongue. The palm of one of his hands smoothed down her thigh again, taking the sheet with it.

Jenny froze. All the pleasant, playful gestures fled. She stiffened. John stopped and looked up at her. "Don't you see? It doesn't matter."

She could only stare back at him, at the flicker of anger that flashed in his gray eyes. He levered himself higher, took her hand and pressed it to his straining penis. "Can't you feel it doesn't matter?"

Jenny sucked in a breath and fought the moisture forming in her eyes. He let go of her hand and kissed her mouth softly.

"Let me show you it doesn't matter," he whispered against her lips.

"John. Wait!"

"Let me show you." He moved downward again, ignoring her feeble attempts to stop him. He kissed her belly, breathing in deeply and rubbing his face across the sensitive skin. He pressed his lips to her hip, the upper side of her thigh, then to the top of one of the scars.

"John . . ."

He didn't look up again until he had traced the newly healed line to her knee. He stopped and ran his fingers over the area, then he sought her gaze.

Jenny had been trying her best not to cry, but when she saw the defiance and determination in his eyes, two huge tears spilled down her cheeks.

With gentle hands he raised her knee and kissed the inside. He advanced upward, but when he reached the inner part of her leg, where her thigh joined her hip, he marked it with his tongue.

Jenny's heart thundered under her ribs as she teetered between embarrassed fear and bone-melting pleasure. She wanted to cry and to laugh, to push him away and to drag him closer.

"I think your leg is fine," he said, nuzzling the very edge of the hair concealing the velvety warmth between her thighs. "Better than fine." He kissed the center of the springy triangle, and his grip on her thighs tightened. "I think it's—" his tongue dipped in exploration "—terrific," he finished, as though he were savoring the word, savoring the very essence of her body.

Every nerve ending in Jenny's body seemed to sing and quake in response. Words were impossible, and suddenly there was no sane reason to cry. She had known pain. She had learned how to control it and survive. But this pleasure was beyond her control, beyond her fear. Captured and driven by John's mouth, John's tongue, Jenny felt a gathering of fire that only required one action—surrender.

John probed and tasted until Jenny was straining and reaching for the next stroke, the next touch. He intended to go slowly this time, to use the opportunity to really make her burn. He pulled her hips closer, delved deeper, until her hands were twisted in the sheets, her body taut with building tension.

"Please . . ." Her voice was breathless. Her hand slid over his and gripped his fingers.

"I know what you want." He continued the sweet torture. But her grip tightened and she moved restlessly, pulling away.

"No, please—!"

John went still. *She wants me to stop?* A niggle of worry made its way through the tangle of lecherous thoughts pounding in his brain. He was having a difficult time with the concept of stopping at that particular moment. He kissed her belly and raised himself over her so he could look into her eyes. She seemed distressed, ready to cry again. But if she said no . . .

"What is it, hon?"

Her hands slipped around his back, pulling him down with an urgency betrayed by the bite of her nails. Darkened blue eyes, bright and tearless, gazed up at him. "I want you inside me. Please . . ." She arched her back. "Now."

The urgent words, combined with the yearning in her provocative blue eyes, hit John like a landslide. One moment he was in total control, the next he seemed to be careening downhill, hardly able to breathe.

The voice of reason in his brain ordered him to calm down, but her hands were forcing him into her, and his senses were singing with the smell of her, the taste of her, the way she whispered his name. At that precise second in time he would have sold his uniform, his next promotion, hell, even his soul, to simply be inside her.

"Wait, Jenny." He could barely hear his own words, let alone heed them. "Just a second." Jenny, her teeth digging into her lip, relaxed her hold long enough for him to reach and fumble with the package on the night table. Then he filled her. They fit together as if they were made for this, made for each other.

John relaxed, then thrust again. This time she met him, giving, taking. The rhythm increased until her hands were moving restlessly over his back, her fingers sending shocks down his spine. He couldn't think about how good it felt; he had to think about making it good for Jenny.

"Come on, baby," he whispered, before delivering a hard, openmouthed kiss meant as a send-off.

Her body gathered and bunched beneath his, quivering on the precipice before exploding into an ever-widening epicenter of sensation. A low, wild sound rose within her and the vibration seeped into his bones. In answer, his own body locked into a climax so intense he fleetingly wondered how strong his heart was. He didn't want to die now. Not now.

13

"I JUST CALLED TO SAY good-night." The familiar sensuality of John's low voice whispered across miles of telephone line. "I wish you were here, with me."

"Me, too." A warming current of memory washed through Jenny's body, mingling with the pleasant haze of fatigue. She straightened her legs underneath the sheets, brushing the footboard with her pointed toes. She ought to be worried, afraid of being hurt, but instead she felt freer, more alive. And whole. She was happy, and that should have scared her beyond speech. All alone in the dimly-lit room, she smiled. "If I was there with you, I wouldn't be much fun." She fought back a yawn. "Too tired."

"Oh, I'd let you sleep," he said. Jenny recognized the mischievous lilt in his voice. "For a while."

"Maybe I snore," she teased.

"All the more reason to wake you up occasionally."

Jenny laughed, then did yawn. "Well, if we don't go to sleep soon we'll both be zombies tomorrow."

"On Mondays I usually leave my office between six and seven." He let the statement hang in the air between them.

"So you could be here for dinner by eight?"

"Yeah. No problem." She could tell he was smiling even though he sounded gruff.

"All right, I'll see you at eight. Good night."

"Jenny?"

"Uh-huh?"

"One more thing. I meant to ask you today, but I was sort of distracted."

"Sort of distracted?" she questioned, pretending indignation.

"Definitely distracted. How's that?"

"Better."

"There's a company picnic this Sunday on Post at Battery Park. I have to be there. Will you go with me?"

A moment of silence passed. He was asking her to take another step into his life. Jenny tried to picture him introducing her to his friends. What would they think of her? "Will a lot of people be there?"

"Most of my men and their families. We call it 'forced fun.' We eat hot dogs, drink beer and play softball."

"I'm not very good at softball," she answered warily, giving him the opportunity to withdraw in case this invitation was mere courtesy.

"Well, I'm damned good at it, and I want you to come and watch me play."

Jenny smiled into the phone. She'd watch him do anything. "I'd like that. You'll have to tell me what to bring."

"Just your sweet self," he said in a voice that sent a rippling flutter through her belly. "I'll see you tomorrow night. Good night, hon."

"Good night."

JENNY SMILED as her nephew tormented a bug that had taken a shortcut over the blanket they had spread under a huge oak tree near the base medical center. She could see Linda coming across the small grassy park toward them.

She leaned toward him. "Here comes your mom."

Sean immediately lost interest in the bug and scrambled to his feet. "Mommy!"

Linda swept her son up into her arms.

"It seems odd," Jenny said as she used her crutch to get to her feet, "sitting and waiting while *you* see a doctor, instead of the other way around. How's everything?"

"Just fine." Linda smiled and tousled her younger son's hair. "Thanks for looking after the terminator here."

"Mom? Did the nurse give you a toy for being good?" He turned to Jenny and said proudly, "I got a whistle last time."

"Let's see if I have something hidden away for good waiters." Linda tweaked his nose. "We better check my pocket." To her son's delight she produced a rubber dinosaur. She put him down, then retrieved and folded the blanket.

On the way to the car Linda filled Jenny in on the progress of her pregnancy. "At least I'll get through the summer before I get too big. When I had Tommy in August, I thought I'd never make it through July."

Jenny smiled at her sister. "Sounds like a pitch for birth control."

"Too late!" Linda spread her arms in surrender before opening the car door for her son.

Jenny watched Linda buckle Sean into his car seat, and chose her words carefully.

"I suppose that's one good thing about being told you'll never have children. No more worries about birth control."

Linda backed out of the open door. "Never say never, and besides, you aren't—" Suddenly she stopped and faced her sister. Her confused expression melted into a wicked smile. "John," she said as she inspected Jenny from head to toe.

"What are you looking for—fingerprints?" Jenny tried to appear indignant.

Linda took her sister's arm and pulled her toward the passenger door. "When did this happen? You have to tell me everything."

"Not everything." Jenny laughed. She felt like a teen-ager again. "I just thought you might like to know—"

"*Everything*," Linda demanded playfully.

Jenny didn't tell her everything, conscious of the three-year-old audience in the back seat, but she said enough to raise Linda's eyebrows once or twice. As they pulled in to the parking lot of the supermarket, Linda leaned over and squeezed her hand. "I'm so happy for you, Jen. You deserve all the happiness in the world."

The eagerness fled from Jenny's eyes. "I'm not sure what I deserve," she said. "But whatever it is, it seems to be all happening this week."

Linda turned the car engine off but made no move to leave the car. "You mean the appointment with the law-yers on Wednesday?"

"That's part of it." Jenny sighed, feeling her mood darken even further. "Randy called. He's coming by to-morrow afternoon."

"Shh...oot," Linda muttered, guiltily glancing to-ward Sean. "What does *he* want?"

"He wouldn't tell me over the phone. He's been out of town on a road trip."

"For a year and a half?" Linda asked skeptically, then retracted her words. "Sorry. I should save my sarcasm for him, not use it on you. So how do you feel about all this?"

"Confused," Jenny admitted. "I don't know what to tell John about Randy or what to tell Randy about John."

Linda drew herself up straighter in the seat. "You cer-tainly don't owe Randy any explanations."

"No. But I owe John. I don't want him to think..." She frowned. "I don't know what to say to him."

"Do you love him?"

Jenny remained silent for several seconds. She thought of how John touched her, how he made her smile. The look in his eyes when he was deep inside her. Then she thought of all the unhappy endings that might unfold for the two of them. He took good care of her but caretaking wasn't love. What could a woman in her situation possibly have to offer a man like John? Not a normal marriage. Not a family.

"I could love him," she admitted eventually.

"What does that mean?"

"If I loved anyone, it would be someone like John." Jenny met her sister's eyes. "But I don't want to love anyone...depend on anyone." The thought of loving John, of losing him, of knowing he was somewhere in the world, perfectly happy without her, nearly stopped Jenny's heart. "I'm not strong enough to lose anyone else."

"Bull," Linda said succinctly. "In the first place you're one of the strongest people I know. If you weren't, you'd still be in a hospital room lying in traction. In the second place how do you know you'll ever meet someone like John again? Or that you'll lose him?"

Jenny had no answers. No one had ever affected her the way John did. Without any effort on his part he could change the outlook of her day by simply walking into the room. The attraction scared her; it was overwhelming, elemental. Very much like love. If she allowed it to be...

Linda gathered Jenny's unresisting hands into her own. "Look, I just want you to be happy. It's fine to be scared, too. We're all scared. John is probably shaking in his boots."

Picturing that image, Jenny struggled with a smile. "I can't imagine John being afraid of anything. He doesn't have to be afraid. He says he's lucky." At Linda's puzzled look she added drolly, "He's led a charmed life."

"He certainly seems to have charmed you. When are you going to see him again?"

"Tonight. That's why I need to pick up some groceries. I'm cooking dinner." In her mind she started to run through the list of things she needed. "Oh, and he's invited me to the company picnic on Sunday. I need to know what to wear, what to bring."

Linda eyed her with renewed interest. "John invited you to the picnic?"

"Uh-huh. He said—"

"This must be serious," Linda interrupted with another knowing smile.

"What?" Jenny's stream of thought halted at the word *serious.*

"A captain doesn't take just *any* woman to a company picnic."

Jenny lost her patience. "What are you talking about?"

Linda paused for a moment. "I don't know how to explain it, but believe me. A captain doesn't take any woman to a military function that he doesn't *want* to be seen with."

Seen with. Jenny's equilibrium took a turbulent plunge. "But what about my crutch? How am I supposed to act normal? What will—?"

"Don't worry about it," Linda ordered. "I'm telling you—" she gave Jenny a stern look "—he wouldn't have invited you if he didn't want you there."

Jenny had no answer to that.

Linda glanced through the car window toward the busy supermarket. "Well, let's get to it." She opened her car door.

A plaintive voice called from the back seat. "Mommy? Can I have some jelly bears?"

Linda looked over the seat at her son and smiled. "You certainly *may*," she answered, then grinned at Jenny. "We're celebrating."

JENNY JUMPED as another loud rumble of thunder shook the house. She glanced at her watch. Seven-thirty. Oh, great. She used one crutch to walk to the window, and pushed the curtain aside. No rain yet, but the storm was rolling in from the west with brilliant stabs of lightning and a swirling wind. John would be caught right in the middle of it.

Rain pelted the window like a handful of pebbles, giving her a start. Then headlights illuminated the glass. Jenny made her way to the front door and propped her crutch in the corner. She was going to do without it for the rest of the night. She wanted to be normal, to be—

An impatient knock sounded, and Jenny swung the door open.

John pushed his way inside on a gust of wind. The shoulders of his uniform were darkened with spots of wetness, and his face and hair were damp.

"Made it!" He laughed and encircled Jenny in his arms. His open palm connected with the door frame, and he shut out the storm.

"You're early. I thought the rain would hold you up."

"Nah." He gave her a toe-curling grin. "I outran it."

Jenny looked into his eyes and felt weightless, wordless. The first time she'd seen him, he had been so serious and formal. Now a smile lit his features and kindled an answering fire inside her chest. She watched, mesmerized, as the smile faded.

One long-fingered hand tilted her face up. Warm lips covered her own for a brief kiss, short in duration but long on intent. He seemed to breathe her in before he pulled back. "Did you miss me?"

A loud drumbeat of thunder vibrated the air and the lights blinked. Graphic memories of the afternoon before tumbled through Jenny's mind. Her face must have mirrored the sudden rush of memories, because John's wicked smile returned.

"Good," he said, relieving her of the need to answer. His arms loosened and he glanced toward the kitchen. "What smells so good?" One of his hands settled at the small of her back, as if he would let her go but only so far.

She wanted to bury her face in the front of his wide camouflage-covered chest, somewhere near the name Braithwaite, and stay there for an hour or two. Instead she answered with a shrug, "Pasta." As if food had anything to do with what the evening was all about. As if by not admitting she'd missed him and thought about him constantly, her fear and the situation between them would remain under control. "It's been a while since I made dinner for company, so I kept it simple. Are you hungry?"

His eyes seemed to bore into hers. "Are you kidding?"

She smiled nervously and took a step forward. "It'll only take a minute to—"

"Hey." He stopped her. "Where's your crutch?"

Jenny waved dismissively toward the corner, hoping he wouldn't make too big a deal of her walking unaided. "I'm giving it a rest tonight." She took another step to demonstrate her ability.

John frowned. Then, making some sort of silent decision, he nodded. "After you."

HALFWAY THROUGH DINNER, the lights went out. And stayed out. The storm rumbled around the house like the final chorus of the *1812 Overture.*

John stared out the window at the driving rain. There wasn't much he could do about the storm or the lights.

"We could have dessert by candlelight."

John turned toward the sound of Jenny's voice in the darkness. A flash of illumination revealed her still sitting at the dining table. On the list of the things he wanted, dessert didn't even make the top ten. He moved in her direction. He'd waited through dinner, an officer and a gentleman. But now he was a man with a woman. In the dark. He needed to touch her, to assuage the fever that had overshadowed his day.

By the time he reached her, she was standing. "Where are those night-sight goggles when you really need them?" she joked. His arms slid around her waist. Thunder rumbled again, and he felt a tremor run through her.

He bent toward her. "People who can't see read with their fingers." His lips brushed her cheek as his hands skimmed up her back.

"Braille," Jenny whispered as he kissed the corner of her mouth.

"You can be dessert," he announced while slowly tasting her parted lips with his tongue.

Jenny sagged toward him and her arms rose to pull his head down. She answered his tongue with her own and he forgot about crutches or gentleness. His hands moved downward, fingers flexing and shaping the roundness of her bottom. He pulled her upward, hard against his chest, and pressed her soft center along the solid, nearly painful weight of his erection. He breathed in her sweet scent, swallowed her gasp of surprise and pleasure.

He couldn't tell her how he felt; he didn't know the words. He only knew that he had to hold her, be with her, bury himself inside her. Without a sound he led her through the darkness to her bedroom, to her bed, and pulled her into his arms.

THE PIERCING RING of a telephone jolted John awake. The sound was so close it seemed to reverberate inside his head. Thinking only to stop it, he answered it.

"Hello?"

Silence.

Exasperation melted into confusion, then to anger. Who the hell was calling him in the middle of the night? John cleared his throat. His voice lowered to command tones. "Hello?"

Suddenly Jenny was leaning over him, removing the receiver from his hand.

"Hello?" Her voice sounded sleepy and soft. John relaxed and put the pieces of reality together. He was at Jenny's. The storm, her bed. Her phone. He squinted toward her in the dim light and realized with a stab of chagrin that he should never have answered her phone.

"What?" Jenny seemed alert now. She sat up and pulled the phone cord across his chest. "No, it's all right." She ran a hand through her hair. "I was asleep." She listened for a moment, staring without expression at the light spilling through the doorway. While they had slept the lights had apparently come back on. "After five, then. It can't be earlier. I've got therapy in the morning." After another long spell of silence, Jenny frowned. "Of course I know what I'm doing, and I don't feel the need to discuss it." She didn't leave space for argument. "I'll see you tomorrow. Goodbye."

Jenny reached over him to hang up the receiver. John took the opportunity to cuddle her and kiss her neck. "I'm sorry I answered the phone. When I woke up I didn't know where I was for a second." She felt stiff in his arms. He pulled back and looked into her eyes. "Are you mad at me?"

"No." She smiled. Her body relaxed, but there were shadows in her eyes. She smoothed his chin and cheek with her fingers. "Now I know what it means to be rudely awakened. That was my ex-husband."

John remained perfectly still. He only blinked once, a true feat since he felt as though someone had kicked him in the solar plexus.

Jenny kissed him briefly, then rolled over him and sat up on the edge of the bed. She switched the light on, then bent to retrieve her blouse from the floor.

"Whoa, wait a second." Before John realized it, he had clasped her arm and pulled her down again. She couldn't just calmly say "my ex called," and get away. "What does that mean?" He gazed into her blue eyes, trying to stay calm, trying not to overreact.

"He's coming to see me tomorrow."

John was speechless. One word screeched through his mind. He managed to get it out of his tight throat. "Why?"

Jenny ducked her head. "I don't know. I haven't heard from him in nearly a year. Then out of the blue he called."

Torn between wanting to forbid her to see this guy and the need to make love to her until she wouldn't want to see anyone—much less her ex—John remained frozen. A dark cavern had opened in his mind, an empty place that would swallow the future if he lost Jenny. He took a deep breath. "Would it matter if I said I didn't want you to see him?"

Jenny's gaze connected with his again, puzzled, searching. She seemed to choose her words with care. "I have to see what he wants," she said, avoiding the heart of the question.

"What if he wants you?" John hadn't planned to say that, but he had to know. Did she want her ex back?

"No chance, Captain." Jenny smiled slightly. "I'm a different person now." She touched his lips briefly with her own. "For the first time in years I feel free, in charge of my life. There's no place for him in my future."

"Why do you have to see him, then?" He wanted her to kiss him again. To explain to him. He needed to hear reassurances that would take away his sudden sick feeling.

"I suppose it's sort of a test." Her finger absently traced his forearm from wrist to elbow. "He has something to say to me, so I'll listen. But I have a few things to say to him, too." She squeezed John's arm. "Whatever he wants is old business. I want to get it over with, so I can go on with my life."

What about what I want? John thought as he allowed her to sit up again. He wanted to discuss what was happening between them, between John and Jenny. He couldn't think of anything else. *What about us?*

She stretched languorously and began to dress. After pulling on her panties and blouse, she reached for her watch next to a blinking, digital alarm clock on the night table. "It's only ten-thirty. Are you ready for dessert yet?"

He tried to smile. He tried to act as if he really gave a damn about the time, or dessert, or the fact that the lights were on. Inside, his guts were churning. He had been so busy worrying about Jenny, helping her see a future, he hadn't considered the possibility she might share that future with someone else. He had the sick feeling this phone call was a signal, a flare in the dark, indicating his luck had just run out.

JENNY WATCHED John emerge from the bedroom and felt a surge of unrestrained joy. He had pulled on his camouflage pants and green T-shirt, but he looked rumpled and grumpy. She wanted nothing more than to put her arms around him and kiss him until he smiled again. The thought startled her. From the beginning he'd been the one trying to bring her out of the dumps. Now she was strong enough to offer comfort. She hadn't lied when she said she felt free. Somehow John had given her that gift.

She moved around the table, picking up the remains of dinner. He stopped her halfway to the kitchen and, without a word, relieved her of the dishes she was carrying.

"I made strawberry shortcake," she said as she followed him into the kitchen.

Still silent, he placed the dishes on the counter near the sink. Puzzled at his uncharacteristic quiet, Jenny reached for the handle of the refrigerator. "It's probably—"

Suddenly John pulled her away from the refrigerator and into his arms. He kissed her thoroughly, trapping her between his body and the cabinets, scattering her thoughts with his urgency. When it seemed as though he would never let her draw another breath, he ended the kiss. Bracing his hands on the countertop behind her, he pressed his face into the curve of her neck and went still.

Jenny, overwhelmed by the emotion between them, tried to get herself together. She skimmed her hands along his ribs. "Is something wrong?"

"Yes," he said, the sound muffled against her neck. His breath tickled her hair, sending a shiver of pleasure down to her toes.

"I don't love him, John. I haven't for a long time."

He rubbed his temple against her ear. After another moment of silence he pushed back to meet her eyes, looking pained and unsure. He loosened his arms as if he was suddenly aware that he had her cornered. "What about me?"

The words hit Jenny like a blow to the chest. Her throat felt tight. He seemed as vulnerable as she felt, and as confused. The last thing she ever wanted to do was to hurt him. She wanted to love him. To take a chance on the emotion she saw in his eyes, on the tenderness she felt in his hands when he touched her. But how could she promise him something without being sure of her own heart, her own fears? Was she strong enough to be the woman he thought she was? The woman he could love? He seemed able to overlook her scars and her limp for now, but what about the future? What about a family?

"Do you have to have an answer right now?"

He let out the breath he'd been holding. His body felt as taut as a wire. "No," he said finally. Cloud gray eyes searched her features. "But I need something."

Jenny slid her hands along his jaw and drew his mouth down to hers. She kissed him with all the feelings and words dammed up in her heart. She kissed him until she lost the power to reason, or to worry.

Then he took over.

14

"WHAT DO YOU THINK ABOUT luck, Drew?"

"I'm Irish. What do you think I think?"

"I mean somebody like me who seems to have run out of luck altogether—"

"Hold it." He put the full weight of his muscular arm against the machine extension Jenny was attempting to budge with her good leg. "I refuse to participate in a my-life-has-been-trashed-by-the-universe conversation."

Jenny sighed and blotted her damp forehead with the back of her wrist. "I didn't intend for it to sound that way. But—" she looked up at her therapist "—don't you think some people are just luckier than others?"

Drew withdrew his arm and shifted her back into position. "You mean born winners versus born losers?"

"Sort of, I guess." Jenny frowned as she stretched her leg to lift the weight. "Except I never thought of myself as a loser."

"Good," Drew said. "Because you're not a loser. Besides, people make their own luck."

"Who's in charge of accidents?"

Drew scowled as if he wanted to shake her. "Look, the accident was a long time ago. Sure, it took some things from you, but you've fought back. If you consider it objectively, it's also given you some things."

"I know." Jenny sucked in a breath before she pushed the bar again. "Linda says I'm stronger. The lawyer says I'll be richer." She exhaled with a whoosh. "My ex-husband has suddenly decided I'm worth a phone call. And John . . ."

"John? Is he the soldier?"

"Yeah." Jenny remembered the anguish in John's face when he'd told her about his brother. She forced the bar harder, away from the machine. "He's one of the lucky ones."

Drew fell silent, watching her work. Then he asked, "Is he interested in spreading some of his luck around?"

"You could say that."

"Seems like a fine idea."

"You don't understand, Drew. I've had a lot of time to think about this. I'm not normal anymore, which I can handle. And I can still help other people like me who got up on the wrong side of luck one morning. I could go back to school, become a counselor for kids, or a therapist like you."

Drew stopped her again. "What, exactly, are you asking me? Whether I think you should sacrifice your life to bad luck?" He swept her legs from under the bar and pulled her around to face him. He put one hand on each of her knees and looked into her eyes. "All these months you've sweated and worked to get better and now you're afraid?"

A lump settled in Jenny's throat and her eyes hurt. "Yes, I'm afraid. I'm afraid to want too much, to care too much and then have someone else leave me."

She took a deep breath and raised her chin defiantly. "I think I've done pretty well at putting my life back together. I can look at tomorrow or next week and feel good about it, but I don't believe in happy-ever-after endings."

"So don't think about endings. You still have a life. The best thing you can do with it is to make yourself happy, make yourself some luck." He straightened and rested his hands on his hips, no-nonsense once more. "It's a noble notion to want to help others, but unless you do it for the right reasons, it won't amount to much. And it certainly won't make you happy." He grabbed the towel draped over the back of her seat and handed it to her. "Come on, let's get your bod into the whirlpool."

JENNY PACED AROUND the living room, chastising herself for being nervous. She'd changed clothes twice, rearranged the pillows on the couch three times and looked at her watch at least a thousand times. Why should Randy's sudden reappearance make her so antsy? She'd dealt with their divorce, hadn't she? She didn't want him back in her life. And he didn't sound enthusiastic to see her—only determined.

She wished she had the nerve to call John. Just to hear his voice, to reassure him and herself that Randy didn't have the power to hurt her anymore—that after this visit she would be the same, feel the same. But she had nothing to tell John, not yet, and it wasn't fair to disrupt his afternoon just because she had the jitters. She could handle this herself. She was strong enough.

A loud knocking startled her. A weight seemed to settle in her stomach. She forced herself to take slow, measured steps to the door before she opened it.

Randy looked the same as he had the last time she'd seen him, Jenny decided. Not so much the way his sun-streaked blond hair was cut or the evenly tanned skin of his face. The similarity came from one fact: he wasn't smiling.

LIFE COULD BE A BITCH sometimes. John crumpled a piece of paper and sidearmed it toward the trash can. Why did

Jenny's ex-husband have to show up now? Just when they were on the brink of truly connecting. The feeling was there, he was sure of it. Jenny would never have gone this far unless she cared for him. Commitment, that's what he wanted. He wasn't sure when or how it had happened, but he'd ceased to think about a future without her. He wanted her to say the words, to take the vows.

He hadn't been lying when he told her that her scars and her injury didn't matter to him. The important thing was that Jenny wasn't like his brother. She wasn't suffering—she'd won her battle. No more hospital. She seemed to get better every day. The memory of her fitting her body to his filled his thoughts. It would be hard to improve on incredible. He wanted a future now with Jenny and maybe a family when she was strong enough.

There were so many decisions he needed to make— about his change of command, about his career. Decisions he wanted to discuss and share with Jenny. Would she consider being the wife of a lifer? If he decided to go back to the Rangers at Fort Lewis, would she move with him to Washington?

It was too soon to assume anything, especially with an ex-husband in the picture. It would do him absolutely no good to make any plans.

John stared at the grinning smiley face someone had drawn on the back of the envelope one of his reports had arrived in. Discipline in the army was going to hell, he decided as he rubbed a hand across his chin and glanced at his watch. Six-thirty. He'd work until seven. It would take him another forty-five minutes to get to her house. Two and a half hours was enough time to talk to an ex-husband. Too much time, if she had asked his opinion. But hey, he was fair. He would wait . . . until eight.

THE SIGHT OF THE FOREIGN sports car in the driveway of Jenny's house ran up John's spine like the tightening of a piano wire. He sat in his truck for a long moment, calming himself. He also wanted to give Jenny and her ex time to realize he was there. He glanced toward the front windows. If either of them cared, that is. He silently counted to ten, opened the truck door and got out.

When the front door of Jenny's house opened, John came face-to-face with the competition, so to speak. Not that impressive, John thought as he gave him the once-over. The guy appeared athletic, a solid five-ten or eleven. Blond with an all-American boyish haircut. John hated him before he opened his mouth.

"If you don't mind, Jenny and I are talking. You'll have to come back some other time."

Did this guy actually believe he'd take any kind of dismissal from *him?* John would have laughed, except at that moment he saw Jenny slumped on the couch with her hands over her eyes. She looked as if she'd been tortured, not physically, but emotionally.

John automatically stepped forward. Mr. Blond-and-Athletic stepped in front of him.

Without taking his eyes off Jenny, John said, "I destroy equipment and kill people for a living. If you have anything more than shit for brains, you'll get out of my way."

"John, don't." Jenny's voice sounded hoarse. "Let him in, Randy." She was looking at them now, at Randy, and John realized she was furious. "I think it's time you left, anyway."

Randy seemed pumped, but he backed away from John and moved toward Jenny. "We haven't agreed on anything yet."

Jenny's eyes were hard. John had never seen her so pale, or so angry. "No, we haven't." A fake smile twisted her mouth. "I'll let you know how it comes out."

"That's not what I mean, and you know it," Randy said, trying to force some issue. "What are you gonna do? Use all the money to buy soldier boy here?"

"Listen—" John didn't know what he was going to do, but he couldn't just stand there.

"Stop it. Both of you." Jenny got to her feet. She pointed to the door. "Randy, if you don't leave now, you can forget any deal between us."

The threat seemed to trip him up. "Fine," he shot back, but he didn't sound fine at all. He stomped to the door in a manly, athletic way. "I'll see you tomorrow after the meeting."

Jenny didn't acknowledge the appointment, but John found himself saying, "Maybe." With one poisonous glare in his direction, Randy went through the door and slammed it behind him.

John took a deep breath and allowed his muscles to relax. He glanced at Jenny. She was staring at the closed door, her face a mask of stone. He moved toward her.

"I'd like you to leave too, John."

"No."

She met his gaze then, and he kept walking. She would have to shoot him to keep him from touching her. She looked ready to collapse, and he was the perfect person for her to fall on.

"I mean it," she choked. The mask of anger began to crumble. Her eyes filled with tears. She took a small step backward.

"I know you do." He spoke gently, quietly. "And I will, as soon as I ..." He slipped his arms around her and pulled her close to his chest. "Oh, Jenny ..." He didn't know what he had intended to say. Words were worthless. Instead of pushing away, she leaned into him, clutched his shirt and cried as if her heart was shattered.

"Tell me what happened, hon." The low, patient sound of John's voice was like a balm to Jenny's frayed emotions. It renewed the threat of tears but for different reasons. How could she tell him? His arms tightened in a hug, urging her to get it out. How could she *not* tell him? No more secrets. She sagged against him, feeling as though she'd reached the end of her endurance. Finally whipped.

His large hands ran up and down her back. "You want to sit down?"

She nodded against his shoulder.

He loosened his grip and guided her to the couch. She didn't look at him. When he sat and pulled her close again, she pressed her face to the collar of his shirt.

"Talk to me, Jenny," he coaxed. One hand touched the back of her head. "Tell me what's going on, so I'll know why I'm going to pound that guy's perfect teeth down his throat."

A shimmer of fear ran through her. He sounded so calm he couldn't be serious. Jenny pushed back and glanced up at him. "You're not going to pound him." The words were more a question than a statement.

His gray eyes were steady but reflected her pain. "I will if you want me to," he said with a forced smile.

Jenny could see he was trying to ease her sorrow. But seeing him made her think of the future, of a dream she'd uselessly been trying to grasp. She and John...together. A stab of confusion and grief nearly took her breath. Wearily, like an old woman, she moved out of his arms and sat beside him, her elbows resting on her knees and her head bent. She might as well tell him. He knew everything else. "I'm meeting with my lawyer tomorrow about the insurance settlement from the accident," she began, blindly studying her fingernails as John sat silently beside her. "It seems Randy saw my name in the legal notices listed in the newspaper. He came over to talk to me first, before he files his own suit." She glanced toward John briefly. His gaze was unwavering. "There was something I didn't tell you about the accident, something about my medical records." She balled her hands into fists, ignoring the rush of new moisture in her eyes.

"I lost a child." Jenny took a deep breath and closed her eyes. There, she'd said it, and for a few seconds she was mentally catapulted back in time. She remembered feeling detached, in shock. One of her fists went to her stomach, as if she could imagine how it had felt to have a child inside her. John seemed to have turned to stone.

"I didn't even know I was pregnant." She pulled a tissue from her pocket and wiped at her eyes. "After the accident, when they told me about the miscarriage, Randy said . . . it was a good thing, that I had enough problems to deal with. But now . . ."

"Maybe he's just trying to cause trouble." John's voice was hoarse and angry. "Maybe he heard that you're doing fine without him, so he shows up to screw around with your life a little more."

Jenny stared down at her hands again, feeling a slight stirring of anger herself. "No," she said, and echoed John's words. "He shows up because he wants some of the money."

She turned toward John, shifting one knee under her on the couch. A new wave of hot tears gushed down her cheeks. "My lawyer asked for more money because of the baby, and Randy feels some of that money should be his—since it was his. . . ."

John watched Jenny fight to keep her composure and for the first time in a long, long time felt truly violent. He'd been half serious before, being macho. The rush of fury pumping through him now, however, was real and vicious. His hands shook slightly as he reached for her, and for a second he was afraid. He had never wanted to experience these emotions again, not after watching his brother die. All these years he had kept his personal pain under control. Now these same emotions seemed to be sweeping away his restraint.

"I'm so sorry," he whispered. The skin of his face felt as though it was on fire. How could he be so furious one moment and then want to cry for her, with her, the next? Was he losing his mind? An answer drifted into his confusion. *No, your mind is fine. You've lost your heart. Now what are you going to do?*

Jenny sobbed against him. He held her until she quieted again and her breathing calmed. John wanted to tell her that he loved her. He ached to tell her that if she wanted babies, he'd give her babies. And he'd stand right beside her through anything life could throw at them. But this wasn't the time. She was crying over another man's baby, one he couldn't help her mourn the loss of. What the hell could he say to help?

"Jenny... Hon, I know it must have been really hard for you." He could easily imagine how it would have been if she'd been his wife at the time of the accident, carrying his child. He would have gone berserk. "You could start over. Get married, have another child—"

"*No.*" One of Jenny's hands tightened against his chest. Abruptly she pushed out of his arms. "The doctors say no. The injury was—" She swallowed and met his gaze directly. "The odds are against me ever having a child."

John's first reaction was disbelief. He wanted to shrug it off, to say, "You're young and healthy, getting stronger every day. What do the doctors know?" But gazing into her pain-filled blue eyes, he saw certainty. She was saying never. And he could tell that having children was important to her.

"Christ, Jenny... If you—"

"That's why the insurance settlement is so large." She cut him off as if it was her problem and not one he'd been invited to discuss. She gestured toward the closed front door. "Randy is on the outs with the team." She sighed. "He plays soccer, and he's worried he's about to be cut."

John let the subject of babies rest for the moment. He could see it was hurting her, and she didn't want to talk about it anymore. She'd been pushed enough for one day, and he wasn't at all clear on his own feelings concerning children. His feelings about ex-husbands were a different prospect, and not very difficult to express. "What did he mean when he said you were going to use the money to buy me?"

Jenny stared at him, uncertainty written all over her face. "It's a lot of money."

ONE POINT TWO *MILLION* dollars. John slammed the door of his truck and headed for his apartment. It was a *hell* of a lot of money. With that kind of money Jenny could do just about anything she wanted to do. With that kind of money she could pack a bag and disappear out of his life forever. She could hire someone to take care of her. Why would she want to marry a career soldier?

He wanted her to need him.

John ran a hand down his face to ease his scowl as he walked up the sidewalk. What a selfish bastard he was. Jenny deserved that money and more.

She couldn't have children. The pain John felt over that fact surprised him. After his brother had died, he'd decided he never wanted children. He didn't want to get attached, to take the chance of losing someone else he loved. Until Jenny. Somehow as she became the focal point of his love, the image of her having his child had grown in his mind. He'd wanted to become part of her, to share in a connection that could never be broken.

The odds are against me ever having a child.

Well, then, he would do without them. He needed Jenny, any way he could have her. And he would tell her that as soon as he figured out the right words. He would list all the good things they could have together. Hell, they could even adopt kids if that's what she wanted.

But not tonight. It would have been useless to try to tell her anything tonight. She was too upset.

He automatically checked the mail in his box, then jammed the key into the front door lock. It was late. He had finally gotten Jenny settled down, coaxed her to eat some soup and crackers that she'd insisted on fixing herself. Then he'd put her to bed. He had felt so helpless. He wasn't her big brother, he was her lover. A man who would kill anyone who tried to hurt her. But he couldn't fight this enemy. He couldn't fight her past. And he couldn't accept the idea of money replacing the love in her future.

She had looked so stricken he'd wanted to crawl in bed next to her, to simply hold her, but he knew she needed time. Time to deal with her past before she could handle the future. And he needed time to come to grips with the chasm that had suddenly opened between them. One point two million dollars—too damn much money.

He slapped the light switch and kicked the door shut. Oblivious to his mood, Deeno snuffled and pushed at his knees until John was forced to acknowledge him with a brisk pat. Then he crossed the room to his answering machine. As he played back the message from one of his former bosses, he had a difficult time finding satisfaction. Short and sweet—there was a place for him at Fort Lewis if he wanted it. If he wanted it . . . John rewound the message and listened to the words again, but his heart was numb. All he wanted was Jenny.

15

"HOW DID IT GO?" Linda asked, sliding her arm around her sister's waist.

They were walking from the elevator to the front doors of the law building in Topeka, and Jenny felt as if she'd just run a ten-kilometer race, without crutches.

"Fine, I guess." Jenny stopped and dug in her bag for her sunglasses. The sun outside looked impossibly bright, impossibly cheerful. It made her eyes burn. "All I had to do was sign some papers and—it's over. Everybody's happy."

"Did you ask them about Randy?"

"Eckles said that since the marriage was dissolved before negotiations for a settlement were started, Randy signed away any right to the money. He can file a separate suit if he wants, but basically, Eckles told me not to worry about it." Jenny sighed as she slipped on her sunglasses. "I don't know . . . maybe Randy deserves some of the money. It was his attitude that made me angry. He wants the accident to finance a newer, faster life-style— as if we won the lottery or something. Me, I'd trade all the money—anything—to be able to go back and change what happened."

"Well, at least the negotiations are over. You don't have to go through a court battle. I think you should take Eckles's advice and not worry about Randy."

"Yeah." Jenny squeezed her arm around Linda, around Linda's baby-to-be, then reached to push open the glass doors. "I can finally start to make some plans, to get on with my life," she said, thinking about luck . . . about John. Money couldn't buy them a future, children . . . a happy ending. The thought of making plans without him sent a slow ache through her. She wished . . . No, wishing wouldn't do either of them any good.

"I WANT TO THANK YOU for last night. For— You've been so good to me."

John's fingers gripped the phone harder as he studied one particular scuff on the toe of his boot. He frowned. This sounded like a brush-off, as if any second Jenny was going to say goodbye. To prevent it, he said the first thing that came to mind. "I wanted to stay with you." He waited through several moments of silence.

"I'm sorry. I was—"

"I know, you needed to be alone." John rubbed a hand over the tense muscles in his neck. "I just wanted to tell you . . . that I missed you. That's all." When Jenny didn't reply right away, worry swamped him. Why did this conversation feel so awkward? Was she embarrassed about crying on his shoulder? Or had something changed between them, and he'd missed it? One point two million dollars could change a lot of things.

"John, I—"

"I got a call from one of my old bosses yesterday," he pronounced, rushing to fill the air with words—to keep her from saying something he didn't want to hear. "He said there's an opening for me at Fort Lewis in Washington."

"D.C.?"

"No. Washington State. You know, wander off and you're in Canada."

"Oh." Was she disappointed? He couldn't read anything into the tone of her voice. He wished for the thousandth time that day that he could look into her blue eyes. "When will you be moving?" she asked.

"Six months, in November. If I decide to take it, that is. It's a good opportunity, but I need to think about it a little more. Check some other options."

"I've always wanted to visit Seattle. A woman I worked with lived there for a while. She loved it."

John felt something inside him ease. "Maybe you should consider moving there." He wanted to hear her plans, know what she was thinking.

"Sight unseen? I don't think so."

"You could always come and visit me." That was as close as he could get to asking her to go with him.

Jenny fumbled with the phone a moment. His casual offer, underscored with intensity, spoke volumes about hopes and shared futures. Long-denied emotions rose inside her, unchecked. It would be so nice to let go, to say yes to everything John could give. To depend on his love and not worry about his sacrifices. But she couldn't say yes, and it hurt too much to contemplate no. "You never know, I might take you up on that."

"Any time, ma'am. I'm at your service," he offered in a teasing manner that endowed the word *service* with a whole new meaning. "Speaking of service . . . You're still coming to the picnic with me on Sunday, aren't you?"

"I said I would." The idea of meeting so many new people, people who mattered to John, was nerve-racking. But he wanted her to go, and it was time to start dealing with the world outside her front door. "I even bought some sunscreen so I don't fry while I watch you play softball."

"Great." He seemed relieved, as if he had expected her to back out. "I have to get there kind of early to help set up, so how about if I pick you up at ten?"

"Fine. Are you sure I'm not supposed to bring anything?"

"We'll grab one of your lawn chairs for you to sit on, that's it. The food is paid for by the Morale and Welfare Fund."

The Morale and Welfare Fund? Jenny smiled. Everything concerning the army was official and had rules. Rules reminded her of John's unruly roommate. "Are you bringing the three-hundred-pound dog?"

"You mean Deeno? Nah. Nick took him home today. It's funny, he drove me nuts for two weeks but now that he's gone, I sorta miss him."

"Enough to want one of your own?"

"No. I have a much better looking companion in mind."

The seductive tone of his voice made warmth gather in Jenny's cheeks. She groped for words. "I guess I'll see you on Sunday then?" Did she sound as breathless as she thought she did?

She must have, because he gave a low laugh before saying, "You can count on it."

THEY DROVE WITH THE TRUCK windows open, the warm wind in their faces. Traffic was light and the Sunday sky was bright blue with only a few puffy clouds gathered on the horizon. They passed a sign that read Welcome to Fort Riley, Home of the 1st Infantry Division. As they took the next turnoff, on the way to Battery Park, Jenny glanced toward John. He had a funny half smile on his face. She felt her own lips curl slightly.

The memory of his mouth on hers, his hands . . . He'd shown up at her front door twenty minutes early. Supposedly to help her get ready. By the time he'd stopped kissing her and touching her, she'd been ready, all right. But she'd forgotten about the picnic. He hadn't, though, and despite her protests had ushered her to the truck instead of to the bedroom.

John was wearing a T-shirt and a pair of pale blue athletic shorts. Jenny's gaze traced the delineation of muscles, a runner's muscles, from his calf to his thigh. Heat rose through her once more, and she had to look away. He'd said he wanted her to think about him during the picnic. To imagine all the methods he might use to finish what they'd started that morning. It wasn't fair. It had been almost a week since they'd made love. Just looking at him hurt. And now because he had stirred her senses into chaos, all she could think about was getting through this day so they could be alone again.

John slowed the truck and took a right turn into a small, paved turnout. Instead of parking on the pavement, he drove several yards along the trimmed edge of the grass and part of the way up a slight rise.

He indicated a trail in front of them. "It's a pretty good distance over that rise to the park," he said in explanation. "I thought I'd get as close as I could."

Jenny opened her door and slid her feet to the ground. Determined to be as normal as possible, she'd worn a pair of comfortable faded jeans and one of her favorite summer blouses, a kaleidoscope of blues and greens. She'd also decided to leave her crutch at home. She knew she could make it up the trail. All she had to do was take it slowly. John met her at the front of the truck carrying a blanket and her lawn chair.

"Ready?" he asked, but he was frowning. He seemed to have begun to wonder sometime in the past few moments if this was a good idea.

She gave him her I-can-do-this smile and said, "Yup."

It was a long walk to the picnic area, a long walk for someone in Jenny's condition. John adjusted his stride to her slower one. Occasionally he pulled her aside to let other, faster, legs go past, or stopped to point out something in the distance. Men were moving up and down the trail carrying coolers and boxes of food, charcoal and athletic equipment. Every single one of them greeted John. "Good morning, sir." "How's it going, sir?" "Beautiful day, sir."

"You're a pretty popular guy around here, " Jenny teased.

John grinned lecherously. "I'm trying to impress you. Is it working?"

If you only knew, Jenny thought, but she said, "I'll tell you after the fifth inning."

There were a dozen people working around the cooking area, setting up grills and covering tables. Soon Jenny was being introduced to the first sergeant, the executive officer—whom John called the XO—and their respective wives. After that, Jenny concentrated on trying to remember names, because she couldn't keep track of who was a lieutenant or a platoon sergeant.

A steady stream of families filed down the trail as John, along with the other officers, started preparing hot dogs and hamburgers or handed out beer and soda. It was quite a job. Jenny offered to help, but permission was firmly denied and she was told to sit on her lawn chair near some of the wives. She hadn't realized so many people would be attending. There were at least a hundred soldiers, wives and children in the area and more arriving by the moment.

"How long have you known the captain?" Theresa, the first sergeant's wife, asked her.

It seemed as if she'd known John for years but actually it had been only a little less than a month—unless she counted the letters. Her eyes drifted toward him. He was laughing at a gibe the XO had made about his ability to cook. As he threatened the man with a large spatula, Jenny smiled and said, "Since the homecoming." Had he really become so important to her in such a short period of time?

"The men respect him a lot," Theresa said. "But better than that—" she smiled "—they like him."

"I like him, too," Jenny admitted, forcing her attention from John to face Theresa.

She laughed in a knowing fashion. "I can see that. It's about time he settled down with the right woman."

The right woman. Jenny's mind froze. Is that what this picnic was all about? She remembered Linda saying that a captain didn't bring just any woman to a company picnic. Was John announcing to the world that he'd decided she was the right woman?

That idea sent an arrow of wistful longing through her. How she wished she *could* be the right woman for John. The longing faded into an ache. What could she say to him if he asked?

Just then a boy about ten years old raced up to them. "Mom?" He tugged at Theresa's sleeve. "When are we going to set up the games? Most of the kids are here."

Theresa sighed dramatically, then turned to Jenny. "Want to help fill balloons with water?"

BEFORE LUNCH WAS officially served, all the picnickers were called into a group. People sort of parted and shifted until, without much effort, Jenny found herself near the front. Her eyes met John's just as the XO announced that the "old man" had a few things to say to them. John had what Jenny considered his captain's face on. It took her a few seconds to realize that *he* was the "old man" the XO was referring to.

Jenny watched his gaze travel from her to her empty lawn chair and then back again, silently telling her she should sit down. Even though she was tired after helping with the kids' games, she smiled and shook her head. She'd remain standing like everyone else.

"Well, I just want to tell you men how proud I am of all of you," John began. "We kicked some butt in the desert—did the job and then some. And you guys deserve all the credit." A few whoops and scattered applause rippled through the crowd. John smiled. "I also want to tell you that we—" he indicated the officers standing around him "—are going to kick *your* butt in softball this afternoon." This was answered by several disguised coughs, boos and more whoops.

When the noise died down John added, "One more thing. I'd like to congratulate Lieutenant Keyhoe on his engagement." He nodded toward the couple and raised his beer in salute. More applause. A few people around the lieutenant lifted their own cans. John brought his attention back to Jenny. He looked as if he was about to say something else, something significant.

Jenny held her breath.

It seemed like an eternity before he said, "That's it, let's eat," and moved directly toward her.

By the time he reached her, Jenny had recovered. Relief had swept away fear. "They call you the 'old man'?"

she teased in a low voice only John could hear as he steered her to the food line.

John gave her a grin that was half embarrassment and half pride. "Yeah, well, sometimes I feel like their daddy."

Jenny glanced back over the huge crowd. "I can see why. You take care of your friends, of your men and their families." She playfully poked his arm. "Even their dogs. I'm impressed. That's a pretty big job."

"I enjoy it most of the time." As they walked past Jenny's lawn chair, John nodded in that direction. "And it's usually not as difficult as getting you to take it easy."

"See what I mean?" she responded. "When are you going to make time to take care of yourself, or of your own family?" Jenny's mouth dropped open. What ever had possessed her to say that?

They had reached the serving line. John stared at her for a long moment, then he gave her a bone-melting grin. "I'm working on it. You interested in applying?"

Jenny's mouth worked but no words came out. John laughed as he moved behind the table, tossed his beer can in the trash and handed Jenny a plate. When she would have taken it from his hand, he held on.

"I'll be over there in a few minutes to eat with you." The affection in his gray eyes made Jenny's pulse race.

People were crowding into the line behind her. She tried to capture the plate again, but he wouldn't release it. She could feel a blush warming her neck. Behind her someone chuckled.

With a menacing smile and a don't-push-me-too-far look, Jenny pulled the plate with more determination.

John laughed again and finally let go.

"YOU KNOW, YOU DON'T HAVE to impress anybody," John said an hour and a half later as he took a trash bag out of Jenny's hands. He handed it to a passing soldier.

"I'm not trying to impress anyone," Jenny said. But she was lying. She wanted to impress herself and everybody else, including John. She wanted to show herself and the world that she was perfectly healthy—or almost. The only problem was, the more she tried to do, the more pronounced her limp became. The more she pretended she was fine, the louder the dull pain in her hip spoke, like an inner voice agreeing with John that she should take it easy.

"Come on." He took her arm. "Even if you were my wife, you wouldn't be expected to work this hard. I want you to sit down and watch the game."

Jenny's back stiffened at the word *wife* before she gave in to the insistent pressure on her arm. She didn't lean into him, even though it would have taken some of the stress off her leg. She wanted to walk on her own. He escorted her to her chair, gave her arm a meaningful squeeze, then trotted onto the softball field.

"STRIKE THREE. End of the second inning. Score tied four to four." Jenny watched as John and several of his teammates high-fived the pitcher. She couldn't remember the last time she'd attended a softball game. And she had never taken such a personal interest in one of the players.

Jenny cheered and clapped along with the other spectators—mostly wives and children watching husbands and fathers. She felt like an outsider, an observer. This was what normal people did, she realized. Normal people loved, got married, had kids and cheered each other on—whether in softball or life. Whether they were lucky or not.

Inexplicably, Jenny felt happy for them, glad that these families had the chance to fulfill their plans and dreams. As for her own hopes and dreams, she couldn't kid herself any longer. John had mentioned marriage in a careful, roundabout way twice that day. It would kill her if he asked. Because she'd have to say no.

Words and tears and wishes welled up inside her like swirling eddies of water, until she was filled—filled with grief, with resolve, with love. It wasn't someone *like* John she loved. It was John.

And now, because she loved him, she had to let him go.

Jenny wanted him to have what these other men had—normal wives, sons and daughters. A family to cheer him on, not a woman with two strikes against her.

When John came to bat in the third inning there were runners on second and third. He gave her a cocky smile before he approached the plate. The wind was shifting, beginning to kick up dust, and Jenny had to squint to keep her vision clear. After letting the first pitch go by, John hit the next one solidly. Chaos erupted as the ball sailed over the right fielder's head. A three-run homer.

Groans and a few choice words concerning the captain's notorious luck echoed around the infield. The officers' team converged at home plate to celebrate as if they'd already won the game. Afterward, John trotted over to where Jenny was seated, squatted next to her and offered his hand for a high five.

"I told you I was good." His smile was electrifying. He'd just run all the bases, so why was *she* having such a difficult time catching her breath? Speechless, she could only stare at him for a moment. He was sweaty and dusty but to her he'd never looked better. To her astonishment, tears rose in her eyes.

"Not bad," she joked, self-consciously blinking her eyes. "Are you sure it was skill and not luck?"

"Whatever works," John parried, but his smile faded. Gray eyes searched her features in a questioning manner. "Is something wrong? Does your leg hurt?"

"I'm fine," Jenny answered as she drew one hand across her cheek to rub away moisture. But she wasn't fine. She was angry at life and at luck, and she refused to ruin this day by bursting into sentimental tears. "The dust is getting in my eyes."

John studied her face. She held his gaze without flinching. She had to, or he'd know something was wrong, with her, between them. Finally he glanced up at the gathering clouds on the horizon being pushed toward them by the same wind that swirled around them. "The rain might finish this game for us," he said, but he didn't seem in a hurry to get back to it.

Someone on the team called his name. "Be right there," he answered, without turning around. One of his large hands moved over hers. "You're sure everything's okay? You're not tired or anything?"

"I'm fine," she repeated, and then looked over his shoulder in time to see one of his teammates get a hit. Thunder rumbled in the distance. "You'd better get back to the game."

IT WAS THE WIND, not the rain, that actually ended the game in the sixth inning. John's team was ahead by two runs. As the thunder grew ominous, people started gathering flapping blankets and rounding up stray children. John went to help Jenny. Large drops were falling sporadically around her as she folded the blanket he'd brought. He cursed himself for not thinking to bring an umbrella, or for not leaving sooner. Some of the men were still on the field stuffing baseball equipment into bags, but almost everyone else had sprinted for their cars.

The rain began to come down in earnest as he reached her. "Leave it," he ordered as he put one arm around her to shield her from some of the rain and took the blanket out of her hands. She couldn't run. He decided it would be faster if he carried her back to the truck. He looked toward the other men and yelled, "Hey, Hardin!" He dropped the blanket onto Jenny's lawn chair. "Can you get this stuff on your way out?" Hardin waved a yes and John turned to Jenny.

"Let's go," he said, and bent to pick her up. To his surprise she pushed away from him. Her smile was strained, and color rose in her cheeks.

"Please— A little rain won't hurt me." She took a few slow steps toward the trail and beckoned to him. "Come on."

John just stood there and watched, baffled. She stopped, waiting for him in the rain. Something in her eyes pleading—

A flash of lightning lit the horizon, spurring him into movement. He caught up to her in three long strides and took her arm. "It's not too smart to be standing in a park during a storm." The color had faded from her face. She looked pale and tired all of a sudden, and John wanted to get her to the safety of the truck as soon as possible. "It'll be faster if I carry you out of here." He pulled her toward him to do just that, and she resisted again.

He didn't know if it was rain or tears filling her eyes. She stared at him as if he were a stranger who had her cornered. He refused to let go of her arm. "What's wrong?" he asked, completely confused. Jenny's hair was already plastered to her face.

"I walked in here—I can walk out," she said. Her forced smile trembled at the edges. Her eyes drifted to the rest of the men, who were now packed up and heading down the trail.

"Jenny, please. You're getting soaked, let me—"

"We're *both* getting soaked."

The difference seemed important to her.

"All right. We're both getting soaked, so—"

She wrenched out of his grasp and started walking. John felt his anger kick into gear. He wouldn't give her a choice this time; she was acting like a stubborn . . .

Jenny seemed to read his mind, because just as he moved behind her to sweep her into his arms, she awkwardly sidestepped in the other direction. She faced him, furious and miserable. "Stop it!" Her voice broke. Soaking wet, with fists clenched, she stepped backward once. "I'm not going to be carried out of here like some sack of potatoes. I can walk!"

"Jenny—" John reached for her, to reason with her, to find out what the hell was going on. Shaking her head, Jenny stepped backward again, once, twice. John saw the dark object in the grass at her feet just as her heel caught it. "Jenny!" Did he yell, or was the noise in his head simply the crack of thunder? It didn't matter. Before he could grab her, she was falling.

JENNY GRITTED her teeth as her back struck the wet ground. She dug her fingers into the mud and grass and waited for the pain. After a long, slow-motion moment her world was filled with raindrops and John's worried face.

"Jenny." She could barely hear him above the storm, as if the wind had stolen his power of speech. Kneeling over her, trying to block the rain, he looked as though he was in shock.

Pain and fear washed through her and she shut her eyes to hide her humiliation. She needed time to assess the damage.

She felt his hands on her leg, gently, only a touch. "Are you hurt? Is your leg—" The pain was higher, in her back; her leg felt normal. She moved her foot and experienced the same ache she'd had most of the afternoon, but no new pain. No bad pain.

Running footsteps trembled the ground around her, and the rain stopped abruptly. Jenny opened her eyes and blinked to clear them. Two of John's men were holding a plastic tablecloth over her like a tent.

"How bad is it? Can we move you?" John asked her.

Jenny swallowed once, fighting tears. *Please*, she pleaded silently to the maker of the storm and the rain, *let me be all right. I just want to go home*. Warm tears coursed through the cool raindrops on her face. She couldn't look at John or she'd lose control completely. She stared at the flowered pattern of the tablecloth. "Just give me a minute . . . I think I'm okay." Gingerly she pushed up on her elbows. "I fell on my back . . . knocked the wind out of me." The pain was minimal, just a strain or a bruise. Maybe she'd fallen on a rock.

Relief ran through her. At least she wouldn't be taken out of the park by ambulance. She extended one muddy hand to John. "Help me sit up . . ." The "please" stuck in her throat. Not because John didn't deserve it, but because she'd really done it now. Pretending to be normal, she had humiliated herself and him in front of his men.

John didn't wait for please or question her judgment.
He clasped her hand and the upper part of her arm and
slowly raised her to a sitting position. When he seemed
satisfied she could sit up on her own, his hand slipped
from her arm to raise her chin. Jenny thought she felt his
fingers tremble. A new rush of tears blurred her vision
as she looked up at him. She couldn't tell from his expression if he was worried out of his mind or furious.

"Are you sure you're all right?"

She could only nod. "I'm s-sorry," she stammered,
feeling as if a dam had broken inside her and everything
she had built was caving in and washing away. One of her
hands curled around his neck, drawing him closer. She
needed to escape, to pick herself up off this muddy
ground and walk away from all these men standing in the
rain pitying her. But she knew she couldn't do it alone.
Not now. She pushed her face against John's soaked
shirt. "Pl-please take me home." A sob rose inside her
and she wrapped her other arm around him, muddy fingers gripping his shirt. She wanted to hide, to sink into
his skin. "Please."

His arms shifted around her and he picked her up,
holding her tight to his chest. "It's okay," he said, a gruff
reassurance in her ear as he started walking. "Hang on
to me. I'll get you there."

THE RIDE TO Jenny's house was silent beyond the sound
of falling rain and the flapping of windshield wipers.
John glanced toward her one more time. She hadn't spoken or moved since he put her in the truck. She sat
slumped bonelessly in the seat, staring straight ahead.

He returned his attention to driving. He wanted to get
her home, help her get cleaned up and into some dry
clothes. Then he wanted to talk.

What had happened? What had he done? The day had been going well, and she seemed to be having a good time. Then whammo! She was trying to run away from him and falling....

John swallowed and his hands tightened on the wheel. All he'd envisioned when he saw Jenny going down was her in the hospital, her leg wired into a metal cast, or her struggling with crutches. She was so fragile. Why wouldn't she let him help her?

The voice of the past prodded him. *Your brother was fragile. You couldn't help him, even when he let you try.* John pushed the past away. Jenny wasn't dying. It wasn't the same.

With great relief John turned into Jenny's driveway. He didn't want to think about the past. It didn't do anyone any good. He needed to talk about today and tomorrow.

"I WANT TO THANK YOU for helping me home and for—"

"I took you out, why wouldn't I bring you home?" John interrupted, for the hell of it. Jenny was sitting across from him in a chair instead of next to him on the couch. That was the first problem. She'd taken a shower and put on dry clothes at his insistence and now she looked as though she intended to send him packing. He wanted to shout at her or kiss her—anything to shake that distant expression from her face.

"I know, but you—"

"We need to talk," he demanded.

"Yes, we do," she answered, as cool as you please.

John's stomach tightened, and his anger fled. He leaned toward her, elbows propped on knees, and stared into her blue eyes, searching for the woman he had fallen in love with. "What's wrong, Jenny? What happened? Everything was—"

"Everything has been great," she said with a false smile. "I'm sorry about this afternoon." She waved a hand in dismissal. "I was tired and I should have asked to come home sooner."

John's attention was caught on "Everything *has* been great."

Jenny continued. "I've enjoyed spending time with you and I appreciate all the things you've done for me—"

"What the *hell* are you saying?"

Jenny blinked but remained calm and remote. "I'm thanking you for—"

"I hear the words." John pushed to his feet. He had to move, to do something. He propped his hands on his hips to keep from grabbing her. "What do they mean?"

Jenny slowly rose from the chair. When she was standing, she crossed her arms over her chest as if she was growing colder. "I'm saying goodbye." Her eyes were suspiciously bright but steady.

Even though he'd been expecting it, John couldn't believe his ears. He stepped toward her. If he could put his arms around her she wouldn't be cold anymore; she would be warm and safe . . . and his.

She raised one hand palm out to stop him. "I'm moving, John." Her voice held a warning note. "I received the money from the settlement, and I've already started to make the arrangements."

John blinked and found that he was gripping Jenny's arms above the elbows. Her skin was as cold as marble. Her hands were pressed against his damp shirt. "Are you telling me that playtime is over?" He willed his own hands to let go, but instead they shook her once to make his point. "Are you saying you can walk away from me—

hell, *move* away from me—with simply a 'Thanks, I had a good time'?"

A single tear slid down Jenny's pale cheek. The silvery streak of moisture made John's throat ache, but it was the only hope he could see. "If you can do that, why are you crying?"

A look of confusion and pain crossed her features. Her voice came out in a whisper. "Because you're hurting me."

Slapping him would have been kinder. He let her go so fast she wobbled on her feet. He swore and turned away. He couldn't stand the wounded look in her eyes. He had to think, to figure out why this was happening. Only two things were different between them. She'd met his friends, seen his world. And she had gotten the money from the settlement.

John tiredly ran one hand along the tight muscles of his neck, then swiveled around to face her. "It's the money, isn't it?" He watched her for an acknowledgment. "Stop me if I'm wrong," he quipped, but held her gaze without mercy. If she couldn't say it, she was damn well going to listen to him say it. "You know what I want from you. You know I—I want you in my life." Another tear splashed down her cheek but she remained statue still. He took a step toward her, carefully keeping his hands at his sides. "And today you saw exactly what my life is like. Real, but not too exciting."

He waited for a moment, hoping she would disagree with him. She didn't say a word. Fury and desolation roared through him. "Yeah, not too many high rollers in the army."

He knew he was losing it but he needed to wipe that blank look off her face. To make her feel as bad as he was feeling—as foolish, as sick, as desolate. He made a great show of checking her over from her feet to her hair.

"We're fine for a little fun. A good time. Right? But when it comes to something more permanent—" The words jammed in his throat. He snatched his keys from the coffee table. His brain was screaming at him to get out of there; his heart was begging to stay. He fixed her with a glare filled with all his fury. "I'm glad I could be of *service* to you, ma'am." His brain won the argument, and he slammed the door behind him for good measure.

Like a sleepwalker Jenny slowly made her way to the bathroom. She swallowed two of her strongest painkillers, then sat on the bench near the bathtub. She didn't think she could survive one more moment of rational thought or emotional pain. She mopped up the tears flooding her eyes and waited for numbness to overtake her.

16

FROM HER FRONT DOOR Jenny waved as her sister pulled out of the driveway. They'd just been to the grocery store. She'd recovered from the fall at the picnic but this was the first time she'd left the house since John had slammed out her front door three days before. Linda had been reluctant to leave, but Jenny wanted to be alone. She knew she could survive anything now, because living through the past few days without John had been beyond hell.

She had to think, to start making decisions. It was time to make her lies to him come true. She had to move, far and fast, before the full impact of a future without him caught up with her. Before her heart managed to change her mind. The money couldn't make her normal again, but it would help her to make a new, independent life for herself. A life without John.

If she stayed away from him, he'd find someone else. A woman who could give him a complete life, a family. The painful reality of imagining John kissing someone else, loving someone else, nearly took her breath away. No. She refused to think about that. She could miss him, but she wasn't going to sit and imagine him with someone else. She couldn't take it.

As she turned the handle to open the door, the telephone started ringing. She hesitated through the moment of silence that followed. The phone rang again. She leaned her forehead against the rough wood, fighting the potent urge to rush in and answer it. The caller could be a salesman, or her lawyer. Or John. Would he ever want to speak to her again after what she'd let him believe? Not likely.

Jenny squeezed her eyes shut, trying to block the memory of the way he'd looked at her before he stormed out. She would give up anything to see him smile again. Anything except his future. If she saw him, even once to heal her heart, she knew she might never be able to walk away. Just as she knew if she went inside she'd answer the phone, hoping to hear his voice. She pulled her hand from the door handle and turned her back to the door.

It was barely ten o'clock in the morning. The thought of another long day isolated in her house, thinking, made Jenny's stomach queasy. Freedom sat directly in front of her. Her car. She hadn't driven it in nearly two years.

Jenny stared at escape, but her legs didn't seem to want to move. She knew it was time to step into a future on her own, but a pang of misgiving held her immobilized. Linda would be upset and worried about her. John would probably say—

No. What *she* thought was all that counted.

The car started on the first try. Linda had driven it occasionally to run errands and keep up the battery. Jenny sat, belted into the driver's seat, feeling as if she finally had gained some control over her life.

"Now what?" she muttered aloud. She thought of John. Wished that she could— Jenny closed her eyes and drew in a deep breath, striving for composure. She'd realized on a day over eighteen months ago that her life would never be simple again. The accident, Randy, the baby—all of those things were her past. She needed to think out her future on her own, no matter how much she'd love to feel John's arms around her. No matter how much she wished she could be the woman he needed.

She shifted the car into reverse. A destination wasn't important, she decided. She would simply drive.

Take the money and run. One part of her mind wanted
out—out of decisions, out of fear, out of pain. She could
take the settlement and move anywhere. She could run
and keep on running until she found... What? What
exactly did she want?

Not the money. Money couldn't give her back her old
life, her child. Money couldn't buy her a future with
John.

She loved him, and he— She had to bite her lip to hold
back tears. Crying wouldn't help, either.

Jenny drove for an hour without stopping. Finally she
pulled into a gas station feeling calmer but no closer to a
plan. As she fumbled with the gas pump then waited for
the tank to fill, she glanced toward the closest intersec-
tion and the street signs. It surprised her to realize how
close she was to the hospital. She shook her head sadly;
it was a pretty sorry state of affairs when a hospital was
her only refuge. Yet even as she paid for the gas, she knew
that's where she was going. She would surprise Drew and
check on her young friend Mark. That way maybe her
own future would seem less intimidating.

"YOU MUST BE Mark's mother," Jenny said as she offered
her hand to the woman seated in the small waiting room.
The colors in the room were bright and the lamps gave
off a homey glow, but the woman looked a little pale and
slightly nonplussed as she shook Jenny's hand.

"My name is Jenny Teale. Mark and I got to be buddies during my stay at Stonemont."

The woman's expression warmed and her fingers
tightened around Jenny's. "Oh, you must be the one who
gave him the puppet."

"Yes, I hope you don't mind. I've spent a lot of time in
the hospital and I—"

"Of course I don't mind." She smiled and gestured toward the couch. "Please, sit down."

"I really can't stay long. I thought I'd stop by and see how Mark was doing. I didn't know he was having surgery today."

"The doctors made the decision late yesterday. He's finally strong enough. The Children's Foundation brought in a surgeon, a specialist, one of the best in the country. Mark's going to be fine."

Jenny smiled. "I'm so glad. It must be difficult taking care of him—dividing your time between home and the hospital."

"It is, but I'll never complain." She hesitated for a moment. "You know . . . Mark is adopted. My husband and I couldn't have children of our own and, well, he's so special to us . . . like a gift." Her eyes filled with tears and she cleared her throat. "Anyway, this hospital and the people at the Children's Foundation have been very good to us. They've kept Mark alive. I would rather spend my time taking care of him with hope for a future than to lose him altogether."

HOPE FOR A FUTURE. Mark's mother's words rang in Jenny's ears as the elevator took her to the first floor. Thinking about the future always brought her mind back to John. Why couldn't things have been different for them? Why couldn't she have found him when she'd believed in happily ever after?

Mark was adopted and happy. His mother loved him as much or more than her own, natural child. Jenny wondered about Mark's father.

How would John feel about adoption?

Stop it. Jenny squelched the tiny flame of hope that kept flaring up within her. She and John were finished. Why was she still grasping at straws?

The blinking floor numbers blurred in front of her eyes as she fought tears. Because she loved him. And she wished . . .

Jenny sighed in resignation. Love, like money, couldn't guarantee a happy ending. Although in Mark's case, both seemed to work. Love had given him a home and parents. Money—from the Children's Foundation—had brought in a specialist to make him well.

Maybe that was what money was good for, fixing problems. If she couldn't fix her own problems, she might at least be able to help someone else. She didn't want to dwell on love any longer. Or on hope. Jenny stepped off the elevator and headed for the pay phone near the gift shop in the lobby with the seed of an idea germinating in her mind. Fund-raising. Before her injury she'd worked to market and promote athletic shoes. Maybe she could put some of that experience to use for kids who couldn't run and play. She pulled out her address book and dialed her lawyer's number.

THE SUN WAS SETTING by the time Jenny arrived home. As she pulled in to the driveway, she was assailed by memories of John's truck parked next to her car. The welcome sight of him sitting on her front step, back propped against the railing, or standing at her door, smiling. Her throat ached. Nights were the worst. The time when she nearly went crazy missing his face, his voice, his touch.

The pain will go away, she reminded herself for the hundredth time. Missing him will get easier. But the small voice inside her wouldn't stay silent. *So why do you feel worse?*

Jenny parked her car and took her time maneuvering up the driveway. She'd walked without any support all day and she was tired. Too tired to disguise her awkward gait.

She stopped at the bottom step and gazed wearily toward the door. Her phone was ringing again. Jenny sighed and made a second decision about the money she'd received from the settlement. She was going to buy an answering machine.

TIME TO GET REAL, JOHN, his anger whispered. *She doesn't give a damn about you, so do it and get it over with.*

With a flick of his fingers, the flame of the disposable lighter in his hand sprang to life. He ran his fingers close to the flame. He was only a little more than halfway drunk, so he could still feel heat. He needed to get numb or burn the pain away.

The flame disappeared when his thumb released the lever. He turned the lighter over and over in his palm, staring at it, as if it might have some message for him. He took another long pull from his beer.

He'd gone out specifically to buy enough beer to properly celebrate what he was about to do. He'd survived three days—nights and days—without Jenny and that was definitely cause to celebrate.

His mouth twisted with an ironic smile. He wasn't sure his men would think so, since he'd given them more flak than they deserved. Hell, there ought to be some special kind of medal for a company that had to deal with a commander who wished he could rip his own heart out, just to stop the pain.

What were you supposed to do when you wanted someone... *needed* someone, and she didn't need you?

He felt helpless, the way he had after his brother died. He had sworn he would never care that much about anyone ever again. Now Jenny was lost to him and he wasn't sure how to go on without her. John rubbed a hand down his face. His mother had never been the same after losing Kenny. Her life had been devoted to him. And after he was gone . . .

John finished the beer in his hand, then tossed the can aside. He popped open another one.

Damn it! Jenny wasn't dead, and according to her she was doing just fine and would continue to do so—without him. Why had he ever gotten involved with her in the first place? He didn't need to take on her problems. He had enough people to look after. Besides, it had all been a lie: the caring, the lovemaking, the letters.

John set his beer can down and straightened in his chair. He pulled a metal trash can closer to his knees, rubbed his palms along his thighs, then picked up one of Jenny's letters and the lighter.

Time to get real.

His hand moved and fire appeared, just like magic. The flame looked brighter, with a trail, like the wavering light from a flare.

Do it.

John's fingers tightened on the blue envelope and brought it closer to the flame. He stared at his own name, written in her graceful handwriting. He didn't want her lies, her dreams— The corner of the envelope turned brown at the edges and a curl of smoke rose. He released the trigger of the lighter and watched the flame lick along the side of the envelope. His eyes were burning from the smoke or from—

"Christ!" He threw down the envelope and snuffed out the devouring flame. "Jesus H. Christ," he said again as he rubbed the stinging irritation in his eyes. In a flash of movement he launched the lighter across the room. It hit the wall with a resounding crack and pieces flew in all directions.

He picked up the scorched envelope and gingerly pulled the pages out. The side that had touched the flame was still warm.

John,
Now I'm afraid. I have tried not to be, but I know how it is to battle for your life. To fight because everything that used to be so easy is suddenly harder than you ever dreamed. Fight, John. Fight for your country, for your men. Don't spend the precious value of your existence, your future, without exhausting every means you have to protect it. You are part of me now, part of my battle—and I refuse to let you go.

I need to hear your laughter, to scrub your back, to watch you sleep. I need to hear all about your days and share the hours of your nights. I want to watch you grow old and still be your love.

Fight, John, for your life, for our life. Come home to me.

Jenny

"Christ," John whispered as he covered his face with his hands.

Dear Jenny,
I swore to myself that I wouldn't do this. But I've found that, when it comes to you, I will do almost anything.

I love you. I had planned to tell you in person, on a beautiful day, in a special moment. Unfortunately, that moment came and went before I had the chance, or the nerve. That doesn't make it any less true. I still love you.

I used to think that love was for other people. People who were brave enough to jump into it with both feet and not worry about the future. I always worry about the future, about things I can't change or control, about losing someone else I loved, like I lost my brother.

But I don't have to save you, Jenny. You have saved yourself. I love you, and I admire you. Being with you is worth the risk, and I don't want to be afraid anymore.

I want a real future, marriage, commitment. Not a fantasy. I'll do whatever it takes to have it. If money is the issue, or living a military life, I can change that.

If you ever doubted how much I want you, give me the opportunity to prove it. I'm not going to walk away from what I feel for you, Jenny, until you look me in the eye and say no.

I'll be in touch.

John

HE WAITED FOUR DAYS to call her, exactly one week to the day since she'd kicked him out of her life. He told himself he would say "no hard feelings" if she said no. He'd stay calm, ask her about her moving plans as any concerned friend would. He just needed to hear her voice, to see her.

He got her answering machine. "Hello, you've reached 555-6531. Please leave a message at the tone."

John hung up and shook his head.

Well, he'd heard her voice all right, and it was damned hard to admit that even the sound of her routine words on the recording had made his heart beat faster. The machine's intervention also made him angry. Was she there? Listening, waiting to see if he called so she wouldn't have to talk to him?

He called back. After hearing the recording, he hung up again. She wasn't there, he was sure of it. And he couldn't leave some sterile message. Now the question appeared to be, where the hell was she?

He dialed Linda and Wayne's number. Wayne would tell him or he would—

"Hello?" A child's voice interrupted his coercive thoughts.

"Hello." John couldn't tell which boy was speaking, so he bypassed names. "Uh, is your mom or dad home?"

"Daddy's outside fixin' Tommy's flat tire."

John had to smile at the image of Wayne, Mr. I-don't-know-a-wrench-from-a-flamethrower, fixing a bicycle tire. He was about to ask the little boy to go outside and get his dad, but he continued to talk.

"And Mommy went to the hospital to see Aunt Jenny."

JOHN JOGGED UP to the revolving door and pushed through. He couldn't remember if he had said goodbye before he'd hung up the phone. All he knew was, he had to see Jenny. He paced over to the reception desk, wondering what she'd done now. And why couldn't she see that she needed somebody to look out for her? And—

"Excuse me," he said to the receptionist. "Can you tell me where—?"

"You're too late," a voice said immediately behind him.

John spun on his heels and recognized Drew. "What are you talking about? Where is she?"

Drew seemed taken aback by John's urgency but he didn't question him. He shifted his cup of coffee to his left hand and pointed down the hallway with his right. "That way," he said. John turned to leave as Drew counted.

"Let's see, one, two, uh, the third door on the right. But it's all over except for the picture taking."

John barged through the third door on the right just as the photographer ordered, "Okay, everyone. Hold the check up a little higher and look this way. Good. Now smile."

A flash went off and John blinked. Out of the corner of his eye he saw Linda and three or four other people as they turned to see who'd opened the door. His eyes, however, were riveted on Jenny standing at the center of the group having its picture taken. Without pausing to reason it out, he kept moving, straight toward her.

"That's got it. Thank you, everyone," the photographer said.

John ignored the surprised look on Jenny's face and the group of people arranged around her as he hauled her directly into his arms. He was so glad to see that she—

"Thank God you're all right," he murmured, feeling overjoyed and confused in the same breath.

Jenny had thought her heart would stop when she saw John open the door. He'd stalked into the room wearing what he called his BDU—battle dress uniform—looking very ready to do battle. As he strode toward her, like a man on a mission, the words he had written in his letter came back to her in a rush. *If money is the issue, or living a military life, I can change that.*

He was a professional, committed to the army. She couldn't imagine him giving that up. She didn't want him to....

I'll do whatever it takes...

A sweet thrill ran through her and she relaxed against him for a few welcome seconds. She'd sworn to stay away from him, but God, it was so good to see him, to touch him.

"I heard you were at the hospital. I thought you were hurt again." He breathed into her hair. Jenny smiled into his shirt. His arms were so tight around her she was having difficulty breathing.

"I'm fine," she managed to respond. She squeezed her eyes shut. *I've been awful,* she wanted to say, *but now I'm fine.* After one more fierce hug, he relaxed his arms slightly without letting go.

Jenny looked up into John's serious gray eyes and lost track of where they were, of what she was supposed to be doing. She couldn't move, wouldn't move, never wanted to be out of his arms again.

"We'd like to thank you one last time, Mrs. Teale," a voice near her said. Much to her disappointment, John's arms loosened and slid away.

Jenny turned, her body on automatic, and extended her hand to Mr. Danielson. "Yes, fine.... Yes. You're welcome." She knew she was babbling but she couldn't put coherent words together.

"You can be sure we'll make good use of your six hundred thousand dollars," the man assured her before releasing her hand. "And we're looking forward to working with you on some new projects."

People around them were filing out of the room. After Mr. Danielson walked away, John pulled her to face him again. He didn't look angry. He looked as though he wanted to kiss her. "What did you buy?" he asked, but his gaze swept across her face and then zeroed in on her mouth.

"A little bit of happiness for someone, I hope," she answered breathlessly. Her hand moved along his back bringing him closer, wanting him to get on with it. She ran her tongue over her lower lip in anticipation.

"I'm leaving now," Linda announced.

Jenny turned in the direction of the sound. "What?"

One of Linda's hands rose to indicate the empty room. She chuckled. "I said, I'm leaving now. Do you want me to wait for you outside?"

"I, uh—" Jenny stopped when one of John's hands tightened on her arm. She glanced up at him, and the unprotected emotion she saw in his eyes made her heart ache.

"I'll take you home. We need to talk."

"N-no," Jenny stammered. "It's okay, Linda. Thanks."

Linda laughed at Jenny's dazed acquiescence, then awarded John with a playful punch in the biceps. "For the record, I'm on your side," she said and left with a wave. "See ya."

Quiet descended after the door swished closed. John's hands slowly moved along Jenny's back, up to her neck and into her hair. His gray eyes held hers as his thumbs lightly traced her chin and his breath caressed her lips. Goose bumps rose along her arms and neck, sending a delicious ache downward through her belly. Suddenly she couldn't hold her eyes open. "Jenny," he whispered before his lips covered hers.

She welcomed the poignant warmth and sureness of his mouth, the familiar smell of his skin, the sound of his breathing, close and uneven. Her determination to valiantly go on alone, to face the future without him, slipped a few millimeters. Instead of pushing him away, Jenny curled her fingers into his shirt, pulling him closer.

He raised his lips from hers long enough for her to gasp a breath and grasp reality. She thought he must have smiled before his mouth swooped down to hers again. He nuzzled and nibbled her lips, then his tongue hungrily explored her mouth. Jenny lost the power to deliberate. Her heart, cleverly disguised as her mind, whispered, *Forget the future. Love him now.*

With a moan born of dread and delight, she opened to him. Her mouth answered his with a carnal urgency, and her hands moved with sensual purpose, gliding up his back, pulling at his shirt.

He bracketed her face with his hands, holding her steady for a rougher invasion of her lips. Heat tumbled through her, escalating. Just as her desire rose another level, John broke away.

"Do you love me, Jenny?" The words were choppy, out of cadence with his breath.

Without opening her eyes, she sighed. "Yes, love me . . ." She didn't want to think, to make any speeches. She arched her neck, her mouth going in search of his.

His hands slipped from her hair to frame her shoulders. He shook her once, slightly, enough to cause her eyes to open in question.

"I said, do you love me?"

Jenny stared at him a long moment. The expression on his face, desire mixed with pain, cut through any dance of words she might have concocted. They'd been spiraling upward, ready to fly, and now they both had to come down to hard, unyielding earth. She couldn't lie to make things easier. The truth was all she had to give him.

"Yes."

He let out the breath he had been holding, put his head back and squeezed his eyes shut. He looked like someone who'd been walking a tightrope and had finally reached the platform on the far side.

Suddenly he pinned her with a harsh glare. "Then why the *hell* are you trying to leave me?"

Trying was a good way to put it. Jenny realized that she hadn't been very successful, since she was, at that very moment, nestled in his arms. She lowered her gaze to the second button on his uniform, sorting through her thoughts for the right words.

"Is it because of the money? Because I'm in the army?"

"No, it's me. It's—" Somehow, she couldn't find the words to tell him that she felt like half a woman because she couldn't have his children.

His arms slid from her shoulders to tighten at the small of her back in an abbreviated hug. "Marry me."

Jenny blinked to clear her vision. "I do love you." She pressed her lips together. "But I can't—" She stopped for several tense seconds. "You should have a normal wife and a family...children. A s-son," she stammered. "And I can't..."

She watched John take a long, steadying breath. "I love you, Jenny, and you love me. I don't care about anything else." He shrugged and kissed her lightly on the lips. "If it doesn't happen, it doesn't happen. If you want a baby, we'll adopt a baby. There are plenty of kids in the world who need parents." His warm hands kneaded the tense muscles of her back, coaxing. "Just promise me the future, plenty of time to love and be together. That's all I want."

Jenny leaned her forehead against his shoulder because she couldn't look at him. She wanted to say yes more than anything in the world. Maybe they could adopt. Maybe they would find a child like Mark. She remembered his mother's words. *He's like a gift to us.*

And maybe they couldn't. Jenny's conscience prodded her to try one more time. "But you deserve someone who's perfect, someone who can—"

"Stop right there." John held her at arm's length. "Look at me, Jenny, and tell me one thing. If I had come back from the war hurt or...different. Would the woman who wrote me those letters have loved me less? Would she have turned me away because I caught a bullet or stepped on a land mine?"

"But I'm not—"

He hauled her to his chest. His arms trapped hers at her sides. The compelling look in his eyes nearly stopped her heart. "You are the woman in the letters, Jenny. Would *you* have turned me away?"

"No." The hoarse but sure sound of her own voice amazed her. Yet she knew now it was the voice of the strongest, most loving part of her, the part she had revealed in letters to a stranger.

"I think I've been in love with you since the second mail call. Marry me." Before she could reply, he sighed and ran a trembling hand over the springy stubble of his hair. "I meant to do this differently." He looked down at her with such love and exasperation she had to smile. "Hell, I don't even have a ring."

Since the second mail call. He'd loved her before he knew she wasn't perfect. He wasn't worried about endings or luck, or babies. He wanted to love her now. Feeling weightless and hopeful and very much in love, Jenny tugged her arms free and encircled his neck. "I've donated half the money from the accident to the Children's Foundation."

The change of subject seemed to jar him, as if he'd forgotten all about the money. After a few seconds he shrugged again. "I don't care." His arms shifted. "I mean, that's great. I've got some money saved—" He stopped as if he suddenly realized she hadn't actually answered his question. "*Will* you marry me?" he repeated urgently.

She laughed then, with pure, promising, heart-swelling joy. "Yes." She thought of all the letters that had started this whole thing. "Would you like that in writing?"

His lips hovered over her smile. "I'll take it any way I can get it."

Epilogue

John,

It seems like years since I sat down to write you a letter. Even after all this time, I find the simple action of writing your name pure pleasure.

I know we've both been busy lately, so I'm taking this opportunity to tell you—in no uncertain terms—how truly happy I am. I love you more now than I ever dreamed possible. And I fully expect to be smiling at you over the candles of my eightieth birthday cake.

Speaking of birthdays, I received a package today from my sister. I'd told her I hadn't been feeling well for the last few weeks. I'm sure the contents were intended as a joke, although the accompanying note was half serious.

She sent me an early pregnancy test.

She's so silly. But you want to hear something sillier? I tried it.

And guess what?

JOHN RAISED HIS GAZE from the letter he held. Jenny was standing in the doorway with an angelic smile on her face.

She waved a tiny wandlike device and announced, "It's positive."

He thought his heart might beat its way out of his chest. After a moment of mind-scrambling silence, John shot her a smug leer and tried to make his voice come out normal. "I told you I was good, Mrs. Braithwaite."

Jenny crossed the distance between them and slipped into his lap, wrapping her arms around his neck. "You sure it wasn't just luck?" she teased.

"Whatever works," John replied, but felt his smile dissolve. What if something went wrong? What if he lost her? He drew her closer and kissed her sweet mouth until she was all languid and soft in his arms. "We need to find you a good doctor and—"

"You really shouldn't worry so much." Jenny sighed against his lips. "It looks like the doctors were wrong about the odds." Her body rose to meet his hand as she pressed it to her still-flat stomach, below her heart.

She pulled back to meet his eyes.

Then she winked at him. "And we feel lucky today."

HARLEQUIN®

Temptation®
IS TEN!

Join the festivities as Harlequin celebrates Temptation's tenth anniversary in 1994!

Look for tempting treats from your favorite Temptation authors all year long. The celebration begins with Passion's Quest—four exciting sensual stories featuring the most elemental passions....

The temptation continues with Lost Loves, a sizzling miniseries about love lost...love found. And watch for the 500th Temptation in July by bestselling author Rita Clay Estrada, a seductive story in the vein of the much-loved tale, THE IVORY KEY.

In May, look for details of an irresistible offer: three classic Temptation novels by Rita Clay Estrada, Glenda Sanders and Gina Wilkins in a collector's hardcover edition—free with proof of purchase!

After ten tempting years, *nobody* can resist

Temptation®

MILLION DOLLAR SWEEPSTAKES (III)

No purchase necessary. To enter the sweepstakes and receive the Free Books and Surprise Gift, follow the directions published and complete and mail your "Win A Fortune" Game Card. If not taking advantage of the book and gift offer or if the "Win A Fortune" Game Card is missing, you may enter by hand-printing your name and address on a 3" X 5" card and mailing it (limit: one entry per envelope) via First Class Mail to: Million Dollar Sweepstakes (III) "Win A Fortune" Game, P.O. Box 1867, Buffalo, NY 14269-1867, or Million Dollar Sweepstakes (III) "Win A Fortune" Game, P.O. Box 609, Fort Erie, Ontario L2A 5X3. When your entry is received, you will be assigned sweepstakes numbers. To be eligible entries must be received no later than March 31, 1996. No liability is assumed for printing errors or lost, late or misdirected entries. Odds of winning are determined by the number of eligible entries distributed and received.

Sweepstakes open to residents of the U.S. (except Puerto Rico), Canada, Europe and Taiwan who are 18 years of age or older. All applicable laws and regulations apply. Sweepstakes offer void wherever prohibited by law. Values of all prizes are in U.S.currency. This sweepstakes is presented by Torstar Corp, its subsidiaries and affiliates, in conjunction with book, merchandise and/or product offerings. For a copy of the official rules governing this sweepstakes offer, send a self-addressed, stamped envelope (WA residents need not affix return postage) to: MILLION DOLLAR SWEEPSTAKES (III) Rules, P.O. Box 4573, Blair, NE 68009, USA.

SWP-H494

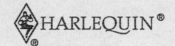

Harlequin Books requests the pleasure of your company this June in Eternity, Massachusetts, for WEDDINGS, INC.

For generations, couples have been coming to Eternity, Massachusetts, to exchange wedding vows. Legend has it that those married in Eternity's chapel are destined for a lifetime of happiness. And the residents are more than willing to give the legend a hand.

Beginning in June, you can experience the legend of Eternity. Watch for one title per month, across all of the Harlequin series.

HARLEQUIN BOOKS... NOT THE SAME OLD STORY!

HARLEQUIN®

MARRIAGE *BY Design*

Harlequin proudly presents four stories about *convenient* but not *conventional* reasons for marriage:

- ◆ To save your godchildren from a "wicked stepmother"

- ◆ To help out your eccentric aunt—and her sexy business partner

- ◆ To bring an old man happiness by making him a grandfather

- ◆ To escape from a ghostly existence and become a real woman

Marriage By Design—four brand-new stories by four of Harlequin's most popular authors:

CATHY GILLEN THACKER
JASMINE CRESSWELL
GLENDA SANDERS
MARGARET CHITTENDEN

Don't miss this exciting collection of stories about marriages of convenience. Available in April, wherever Harlequin books are sold.

MBD94

This June, Harlequin invites you to a wedding of

Promised Brides

Celebrate the joy and romance of weddings past with PROMISED BRIDES—a collection of original historical short stories, written by three best-selling historical authors:

The Wedding of the Century—MARY JO PUTNEY
Jesse's Wife—KRISTIN JAMES
The Handfast—JULIE TETEL

Three unforgettable heroines, three award-winning authors! PROMISED BRIDES is available in June wherever Harlequin Books are sold.

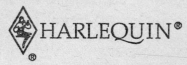

HARLEQUIN®